A
Woman's
Love

A
Woman's
Love

PÁDRAIG STANDÚN

POOLBEG

First published as Cion Mná in 1993 by
Cló Iar-Chonnachta, Indreabhán, Contae na Gaillimhe, Éire
The English edition, translated by the author, published in 1994
by arrangement with Cló Iar-Chonnachta, by
Poolbeg
A division of Poolbeg Enterprises Ltd,
Knocksedan House,
123 Baldoyle Industrial Estate,
Dublin 13, Ireland

A catalogue record for this book is available from the British Library

ISBN 1 85371 346 5

Cover photograph by Peter Maybury
Cover Design by Poolbeg Group Services Ltd
Set by Mac Book Limited in Stone 10/13
Printed by Cox & Wyman Limited
Reading, Berks

A NOTE ON THE AUTHOR

Pádraig Standún was born near Castlebar County Mayo. He has been a priest for twenty-two years in Connemara and the Aran Islands. *A Woman's Love* is his third novel to be published by Poolbeg.

Bridie was getting their dinner, checking the sitting-room every now and again to make sure that Caomhán wasn't tearing something asunder. He was at the stage when everything had to be investigated, searched, taken apart. On this occasion he sat looking at Bosco on the television.

It seemed to Bridie to be the same Bosco interminably repeated year in, year out, the puppet and the programmes looking the same, only the children growing old. She wondered why the national television station could not come up with something new. She also recognised its effectiveness in keeping Caomhán's attention.

"Never mind," Therese would say as his mother tried to prevent him pulling out the contents of a cupboard. "It's all part of his education." How would she like it if her Waterford glass was in smithereens on the floor? In fact, she probably wouldn't mind, Bridie thought. Shortage of money certainly wasn't one of her problems. Still, nobody could say she was mean. If anything it was too good that she was to Caomhán. She had him spoiled rotten. You'd think sometimes that he was her own. As good and all as Thatch was at her job, maybe she missed motherhood.

Bridie sat at the big pine kitchen table and lit a cigarette to have with her coffee. She would be able to see Caomhán through the open double doors and keep an eye on the dinner at the same time. Apart from preparing the meat and vegetables there was nothing easier or safer than a casserole. It didn't spoil if someone was a little late and it was the type of dinner Therese enjoyed after coming from a tour of the building sites, or before going out to a meeting in some cold community centre.

She'll be free tonight, Bridie thought, but you'd never know. A crisis somewhere might need her calming influence, her incisive mind, her ability to iron out problems. But with a bit of luck she would have a night off, a bottle of wine with dinner, their shoes kicked off in front of the great open fire, classical music, conversation until midnight. Much as she loved her child, Bridie felt the need of adult company after a day changing nappies, cleaning, minding, watching. Always watching. You never knew what he was going to get up to next.

Caomhán came into the kitchen. He dragged himself up on her knee, hugged and kissed her. Then he laid his head on her shoulder. "Caomhán is tired," Bridie said, "Caomhán is hungry. Get your teddy, and we'll have a cuddle until Therese comes home. Dinner will be ready then."

"Teetie sweetie," he said, before sliding down out of his mother's arms and going to collect his battered teddy bear.

"I think Caomhán needs to be changed." Bridie held her nose in an exaggerated fashion as he climbed up on her knee again. He laughed at her playacting, shaking his head from side to side, holding his own nose then as well. "I'll have to change you before dinner," she said, "or the smell will be worse than that goulash in the pot. Therese won't know which is which."

She hugged her child to her. "A little cuddle first, and then the nappy." Caomhán held his cheek against hers as he began to suck on his thumb. He was her whole world, Bridie thought. What would she do without him? If anything was ever to happen him she knew that she would go soon after him. She had thought once that when he got past the danger of a cot death she'd have peace of mind. Since he started to walk danger lurked everywhere, the fire, the steps in front of the house, the electric plugs, the cooker, the bath, everything. Still, children managed to survive, somehow.

He was the best thing that had ever happened her. It was hard to believe that she had hated him when he was in her womb. How much trouble he had brought her then, marriage, beatings, batterings, rape. Rape it was too, though John had called it his marriage right. She tried to put John out of her mind, there were too many bad memories. She didn't want to put herself in bad form before Therese came home. Thinking of her husband tended to have that effect on her, so she tried to blot out the time they had spent together.

She wondered how he was. She hated him and pitied him at the same time. She didn't know how she should feel when she reminded herself that he was Caomhán's daddy. His son looked so much like him it would make you want to cry. She didn't know how she felt really. One thing sure, she wouldn't have anything to do with any man again. Ever.

Was she to spend the rest of her life looking after somebody else's home, she asked herself, another woman as her boss? Not that Therese did any bossing, but she wasn't her own boss either. Some day they would have a home of their own, when Caomhán gets on his feet properly...

Bridie saw clearly in the eyes of her mind the house they would have in a couple of years. A two-bedroomed house in Galway, not far from the University, so that it wouldn't cost much for Caomhán to go there when he was older. She herself would work as a secretary in some financial institution. She meant to do a course in computers when he started school. A pity she hadn't finished school when she had the chance. But no use crying over spilt milk. She was young yet, and Therese had promised to give her all the help she could.

If she managed to get a bigger house, Bridie mused, she'd be able to keep lodgers, students or nurses in the winter, holidaymakers in the summer. She was a good cook and unlike many women she knew she actually liked housework. Not that anyone is ever remembered for housework, she told herself, but she had no hang-ups about it. Caomhán would help out, help her prepare the breakfasts for the tourists in their Bed and Breakfast as he was growing up.

Where was the money to come from? God is good, and he has a good mother, she remembered the old Irish prayer. "Not that either of them did very much for me," she thought, immediately chiding herself for finding fault with God. "A right one, I am, that hasn't said a prayer in an age."

She had missed Sunday Mass twice in a fortnight. But what was she to do? Caomhán made a lot of noise, and the old priest was inclined to be contrary in the mornings. His parishioners blamed it on drunken hangovers. Whatever it was he certainly didn't like to have his sermon disturbed by rowdy children. "They had an ass in the stable at Bethlehem too," he would say when there was a bit of a racket, and of course all eyes would turn to the noisy child and its mother.

"Excuses, excuses. Blame everyone except myself," she thought. Therese would mind him, no bother, if she asked. Therese never darkened the door of church, chapel or meeting place. At the same time she'd have great crack with the priests at factory official openings, threatening to blame their blessings if the business went to the wall. "You're a funny one all right," Bridie smiled as she thought how full of contradictions her friend was. "Employer," she reminded herself. "You don't work for money for your friends."

Hardly a Sunday passed that Caomhán didn't climb into bed beside Therese, tearing newspapers from her grasp until he had her full attention. She had great patience with him. She would tickle him and wrestle with him until the bedclothes joined the papers on the floor. She put up with a lot from him really, Bridie thought, but then she didn't have to look after him from morning till night seven days a week.

Bridie felt that she'd landed on her feet ever since she answered that advertisement. She still remembered buying the *Connacht Tribune* in Kilburn High Street. She could barely afford it but she was so homesick that she wanted to read something, anything about home, Galway, Connemara. The small ad had caught her eye, an answer to prayer? She was too proud to go home unless she could be independent of her parents and this seemed almost like an invitation. She just had a feeling about it, a good feeling. "So what if I don't get it," she had told herself, "at least it's the right idea, an opportunity to earn some money and be with Caomhán at the same time. If I don't get this one I'll try for something similar."

She had wanted to be far away from London when John got out of prison. Two years he got for the battering he gave her the night the baby was baptised. He lost the head completely. The police were sent for when she was found wandering about concussed, bruised and bloody near the bottom of the stairwell. He had thrown her bodily out of the flat, not caring where she was to land. The doctor told her she was lucky to be alive.

John was asleep when the police had forced open the flat door, unaware apparently of the damage he had done. That was his story anyway and she was inclined to believe it. When he got into that kind of drunken frenzy he seemed to lose control. The social worker told her it was common enough for a violent alcoholic to forget what he had done. "Thank God," Bridie said to herself, "that he never laid a hand on the child." In fact John treated his son like a precious toy doll that might break in his hands, but then the child was only five or six weeks old when he was christened. There was no knowing what might have happened when he was older.

John could be so full of anger that you would never know what he might do. He was so strong that he would kill the child with a swipe of his hand. But she'd kill him if he laid a hand on Caomhán. She had no doubt about that. As she thought about it she held her son even closer. "Come on, young fellow," she said to him, "I'd better get you cleaned up before dinner-time." She carried him into the sitting-room and he had great fun as he was changed on the sheepskin in front of the fire, powder flying in all directions from the Johnson box in his hands.

❦

It was an easy meeting. Small amounts of grant aid were being discussed, the Government-appointed members of the Gaeltacht Board trying to save money, the elected members trying to spend it. So be it. That would satisfy their constituents. It was the elected members' support Therese would need when there were serious matters to be decided at a later date.

Therese did not say much at any meeting. She left the talk to the committee members. It was action that she was interested in. She had proven herself in the business field in England long before returning to the West of Ireland. Since taking up her appointment as Chief Executive of the Gaeltacht Board, she had shown what an effective and far-seeing person she was. The easing of the recession had helped, of course, but she was seen locally as the right person in the right place to catch the rising economic tide.

Everyone in the offices of the Board and many outside knew her as "Thatch." She herself was aware of her nickname, but did not know whether it was because of her thatch of short blonde hair, or because many compared her to Margaret Thatcher. She didn't care where the name had come from. In fact she liked it so much that she sometimes signed it on office memos to annoy the more prim and proper officials.

Some of the senior civil servants in the organisation thought that she lacked dignity and was far too familiar with the workforce. Therese clearly enjoyed visiting building sites, where she engaged in slanging matches with the workmen, often using language calculated to shock her officials. She knew it was good for morale. The men loved her, and would do anything

for her, including working unseasonable hours to get
a particular project finished. And Therese saw to it that
they were more than adequately rewarded, not just
financially, but with extra time off.

"Sweets for Caomhán," was the only thing written
on the notepaper in front of her. Hardly an evening
passed that Therese did not bring sweets home to
Bridie's little boy. She knew Bridie did not approve, so
she sometimes gave the gifts to Caomhán unknown to
his mother. "To hell with the baby teeth," Therese
would say, when the little fellow let out their secret.
"Won't a new set grow when he's seven. I can't refuse
anything to my big *peata*." She would hug him. Bridie
would say resignedly, "Would you look at herself that
has the reputation of being as hard as a rock?"

Therese awoke from her daydream to answer a
query about mussels being farmed in Casheen Bay. It
gave her an opportunity to announce a large Japanese
order for processed shellfish, with the prospect of
selling farmed salmon to the same customer. "If we
can get a proper foothold with quality fish products in
that market," she said, "the sky's the limit. All the
investment in research in the past twenty years is
money well spent." Nothing pleased the Board
members more than this kind of backhanded
compliment for being so far-seeing in the past.

Towards the end of the meeting she gave a
comprehensive report on her plans for an independent
Irish language television service. This was intended to
complement the couple of hours per day of
programming on the Third Channel introduced in
the mid nineties. Therese explained that it would be
funded first of all by advertising revenue. There would
be a doubling of the ordinary TV licence for everybody

availing of the service, and a home bingo game that could be played by digital telephone. "I'd hope," Therese stressed, "that programmes would be so good that subtitled and dubbed versions could be sold to television services around the world. There's a great interest globally in minority language programmes as an antidote to mass-produced lowest common denominator stuff beamed around by the satellites."

Discussions and arguments started among the Board members, particularly about the cost of the licence. The bearded Independent from South-west Connemara complained that it would be grossly unfair for people to be punished for speaking the language of their forefathers. "First it was beaten out of the people," he said, "now it's being made too expensive for them. Is this aimed at the ordinary people or at the big bucks above in Dublin? Irish is just a passing fashion for them."

"I'm convinced, not just from my own observations," Therese replied, "but by my market research, that people will pay extra for quality, and for what their hearts desire in terms of culture. Interest in Irish in the cities is far more than a fashion now. People are prepared to put their money where their mouths are, literally. This new development would also mean, of course, that Teilifís na Gaeltachta would be absolutely independent of Government interference."

"Does that mean that Sinn Féin and the IRA will have a free rein to publicise their murderous activities through the medium of the first official language?" the Fine Gael member from Donegal asked.

"I don't believe in censorship," Therese replied. This gave rise to heated debate which had lasted nearly half an hour when the Chairman adjourned the meeting. An independent Fianna Fáiler had refused to withdraw the "bloody Blueshirt" epithet he had applied to his Fine Gael countyman. It was nothing new for an argument to go off on that kind of a tangent.

Apart from that localised disagreement which had more to do with the past than with the future, there seemed to be general approval of the plan. Therese was delighted. She felt that she would succeed once again against the odds. "A born competitor," she thought. She was going to live up to the Midas touch, golden-fingered reputation she had established for herself since taking up her present position.

Caomhán was on his high chair eating his dinner when Therese came home. "Hi," she said. She kicked each shoe in a different direction as she did every evening as soon as she entered the house. A scarf, handbag and folder were dropped in a trail as she headed over to hug Caomhán. His food smudged her lips but she just wiped it off and licked her fingers. For a woman with a reputation for being highly organised Bridie had never seen anyone so untidy. "Isn't it all right for her," she told herself with more than a little venom, "her servant girl here to pick up after her."

"Meetings, meetings..." Therese flopped into one of the easy chairs. "You're so lucky, Bridie, that you never need to attend a meeting. They'd drive you mad; those politicians never see beyond the end of their own red noses. They always have at least one eye on the next election."

"Anything'd be better than housework and changing nappies all day long." Bridie helped Caomhán to gather up the food he'd scattered all over the tray of his high chair with his little plastic knife and fork. "They say a woman's work is never done. Some women. At least yours finishes at five."

"An odd day. How many nights am I out at meetings and functions until the early hours of the morning?"

"More pleasure than business, you must admit."

"I get so fed up with it. When you've seen one of those functions, Bridie, you've seen them all."

"I'll swop with you any time." Bridie was showing Caomhán how to use the little knife and fork, trying to get him to finish his dinner. "You have the time of Reilly, out getting pissed most nights."

"It's all for Ireland," Therese laughed. "Some die for it, others just get hungover."

"This little man is impossible to feed." Caomhán had his arm across his eyes playing "hidies" with Thatch as his mother tried to feed him. She was afraid he'd stick the plastic fork, blunt and all as it was, in his eye.

"Let Teetie help him." Therese got a spoon and put some of his dinner on it. She pretended she was going to eat it herself, which brought peals of laughter from the boy. Making a noise like the chug-chug of a train she brought the spoon to his mouth. She kept up the game until most of his dinner had been eaten.

"Leave him be. Your own meal will be cold." Bridie had finished serving and was sitting down to her own dinner.

"He'd never manage it with that little knife and fork."

"He'd get the hang of it if he was allowed practise long enough," Bridie said. She relented a little when she saw that most of the food had gone. "I suppose the main thing is that he's eaten it."

"And Teetie has something for a big boy that ate all his dinner." She pointed to her bag on the floor.

"Sweetie." Caomhán lifted up his arms to be taken out of the chair.

"When everyone's finished their dinner." Bridie laid down the law. She'd have no comfort at all with her own meal if he was running around, rifling Therese's bag, scattering her make-up all over the floor.

"There's a bottle of plonk in my bag, Bridie." Therese pointed at it. "Good plonk, they say, if that's not a contradiction in terms. Would you ever open it, like a good girl?"

Bridie had it on the top of her tongue to say, "Open it yourself, if you want it," but she held her tongue. "The less said the easier mended," her father used to say. That was the worst of working for someone else, she thought. You can't just tell them to go and fuck themselves.

"Thank goodness I have no meeting tonight. Is there much on the telly?" Therese took a mouthful of dinner, reached quickly for the glass Bridie had just filled, and drank deeply to cool the hot food on her tongue. "Do you know, that stew is as nice as I've ever tasted, really lovely."

"We call that goulash at home," said Bridie with a little irony.

"Sorry about that, but what's goulash anyway, but Hungarian stew? Just the same as we have Irish stew here in this country."

"It all depends on what you put in it."

"It's all the same to me, that cannot even boil an egg. Wasn't I the lucky woman to get such a good cook?"

"You mightn't have her for much longer."

"You're not thinking of leaving me?"

"I have to think of my own future."

"But aren't you all right here, and Caomhán couldn't be happier?"

"There's more to life than rearing children, and anyway, they don't remain children for long."

"Sure he's hardly two years old yet."

"I have to think of myself as well," Bridie said.

"I'd hate to see you going. Either, both of you. And it's not on account of the food. Sure I'd be lost without my little doteen here." Caomhán was using his upturned plate as a drum for his knife and fork.

"Can't you have a little one of your own?" Bridie said drily.

"Another immaculate conception?"

"Sure you don't give a chance to any man. You're great with them all, but you don't stick with any of them long enough to get to know them right." She rose to wipe Caomhán's hands and face with a damp towel. He had goulash to his elbows and ears. "There are plenty of fish in the sea," she said to Therese.

"Every one of them fishier than the next," Therese joked.

"Not every fish is a shark either."

"It's time for this foolish old virgin to stop thinking of that old crack."

"You're neither old nor foolish, and I'd be inclined to have my doubts about the other thing as well, somehow. I have a feeling that there aren't too many of those around in this day and age, unfortunately."

"Why the unfortunately?"

"Well, I'm sorry I didn't hold on to my own, for another while anyway. I wouldn't be where I am today... Anyway life was a lot better when standards were higher. I'm going to look for my own back."

"Your own what?" Therese didn't know if she'd lost her or not.

"My virginity," Bridie giggled as she rose to do the dishes. She felt relaxed and light-headed after the wine. She kissed Caomhán as she lifted him from his high chair. "But I wouldn't have you if I hadn't lost it," she said.

"Leave the dishes." Therese was enjoying the banter.

"I'd prefer to have them out of the way, and just flop in front of the television when I've this fellow bathed and in his bed. It's a long day trying to keep up with him from morning till night."

"I'll wash them. I should have a dishwasher anyway. It'd make life easier."

"You have one already," Bridie joked, "me."

"Well, I'm doing them myself tonight."

"What's got into you all of a sudden?"

"I'd do them, or at least help with them a lot oftener, if you weren't always in such a hurry. I get heartburn if I start fussing about too soon after a meal. Sure most evenings I only have time for a bite before going out to a meeting. We're in no hurry tonight and I'd much prefer to keep up the chat we're having, but the banging and clattering always starts when the conversation gets interesting."

"It can get too interesting," Bridie said matter-of-factly, "raking over the past is no help to anyone."

"I thought it was all very light-hearted."

"Things like that tend to get too deep. People say too much, say things they didn't mean to say." Bridie wasn't finding the right words. "There are certain things best kept to yourself, especially..." She fell silent.

"Especially?" Therese prompted.

"You don't have to tell every single secret you have to the person you're working for," Bridie blurted out.

"I hope we're a bit closer than employer and employee."

"You can never really be best mates with the person you're working for." Bridie stood with her arms folded, looking everywhere but at Therese. "Anyway, sure you're out nearly every night, at meetings half the time, and in the pub until all hours."

"Why does this keep coming up? Do you think I have a drink problem?"

"Don't be daft," Bridie said.

"It's part of my job. Mostly it's meetings, but there's a social side to it too. I have to keep in touch with what's going on, keep my ear to the ground."

"What a pain in the arse that must be," Bridie said, with a twinkle in her eye.

"I much prefer a night like this when the three of us are here together. And I love the Sundays that we go back for a spin through Connemara or down to the Burren. I do enjoy your company, Bridie, and of course I'm cracked about your man here. I think of the three of us as a unit, a little family, and I hope it stays like that."

"'We're all the one, and I'm the one'," Bridie quoted an old joke her father used to tell about a couple who had just married. "You're all the one now," the priest had told them at the ceremony. "We're all the one now," the bride said afterwards, "and I'm the one."

"Are you trying to tell me I'm domineering?" Therese asked.

"It's pretty clear who's the boss."

"It must be habit, from the job." She shrugged her shoulders, surprised to find she came across like that. "Well, pull me up, remind me when I'm bossy. It'll be good for me." She noticed that Bridie had a smirk on her face. "What is it? What smart one are you going to come out with now?"

"Sure you're always bossy. You couldn't be anything but bossy. It would be against your nature."

"Am I that bad?" Therese asked seriously.

"I'm not complaining."

"Sounds like it to me."

"It's not your fault. It's the way things are. I depend on you for everything, you don't need me for anything."

"I'd live like a pig in a pigsty only for you," Therese said. "I can't cook. I can't sew. I don't even see dirt when I try to clean up a place."

"You don't see my point." Bridie put her hands up to the sides of her head in exasperation. "You pay me to do those things. Any woman could do them. Any man for that matter. They could, but they probably wouldn't. You don't depend on me for anything." She held out her hands. "You just buy my services."

"I pay you because you do a good job, because you need the money, whatever the reason. I don't buy you, don't own you. It shouldn't stop us from being friends."

"Friends. I couldn't even call you by your name a minute ago," Bridie admitted, "even though I wanted to."

"What stopped you?"

"Respect, I think. I don't know."

"Respect me arse. It's me you're talking to now, and my name is Therese. Therese. Say it. Repeat after me..."

"You're mocking me now, as well as bossing me."

"I give up," Therese said. "What is it you want?"

"I don't know. Respect, maybe."

"Respect?"

"To be treated equally, treated the same."

"Don't I do that?"

"Everyone needs their own independence," Bridie replied. "Sure I depend on you even to go out for a spin."

"So what? I enjoy it as much as you do." Therese didn't grasp how deeply Bridie felt about her position.

"I know that a woman with a child, married or single, is never completely independent, and I'm not complaining about that. It's just, well, it's just that you're up there, a good job, satisfaction in your work, praised by everyone. I've nothing like that in my life. I'm nothing."

"What kind of talk is that? Sure what am I either, or anyone else?"

"But you've done something with your life, achieved something."

"Haven't you done something very important with your own life? You wouldn't swap Caomhán surely for what I have, or what you think I have? When you've reared your child you'll have done far more with your life than all the factories I'll have opened all over the Gaeltacht. Half of them will close down again, if the past is anything to go by. I'm just a functionary. A good one mind, but still a functionary. Who'll remember me for that the way your son will remember you?"

"Sure he might hate me when he grows up."

"Sure he might. Sure he mightn't. Sure he might anything. That's a chance you have to take." Therese finished the dishes and swept the floor as Bridie readied Caomhán for bed. He ran around for a while, going from one to the other, enjoying the attention he was getting. He eventually settled in his mother's arms, his thumb in his mouth, a little teddy bear under his arm. She put him into his cot as his eyes were closing. The two women sat down then to watch an American detective series on television.

"I've a feeling that I've seen this before," Bridie commented after a while.

"Sure they're all the same anyway."

"It's amazing the amount of money they waste, fancy cars being blown up, helicopters being shot down. It must cost a fortune to make."

"They must get every penny back or they wouldn't keep making them, *amadáns* like us foolish enough to waste our time looking at them."

"Sure they pass a while of the night." Bridie took up her knitting, glancing at the television from time to time.

"That's what we were talking about at the meeting this evening."

"Drugs?" Bridie thought she was talking about the programme.

"No, but television." Therese explained her own ideas for an independent Irish language TV service. She didn't mention the reaction of the politicians or the heated exchanges. The meetings were supposed to be confidential. This seldom stopped "sources close to the Board" from revealing all to local reporters, but as Chief Executive Therese never revealed anything except generalities.

Bridie lost interest in her explanation inside a minute, although she nodded her head now and again

as if she was paying attention. She was thinking of
John, wondering when he'd be let out of prison. A year
and a half someone had said, if he kept the rules, was
of good conduct. John would keep the rules all right,
be a little saint in a place like that. Hitting a woman
was a different matter. She had to laugh when Therese
interrupted her reverie. "You haven't heard a word I
said."

"My mind had gone for a wander."

"Where to?"

"I was thinking of my husband, believe it or not."

"I thought you wanted to forget him."

"I do too. Who was it said that the past is another
country?"

"Still, I suppose he is Caomhán's father."

"Some father," Bridie remarked sourly. "What does
father mean, that it was he that did the job? That's
about all he did do right."

"Is he still in London?"

"He should be out soon."

"Out?"

"I thought everyone around here knew where he
was. Our father who art in jail," Bridie said, bitterly.

"You never told me that."

"I suppose I was too ashamed, though I don't know
why. Some kind of protective instinct, thinking I'd be
letting myself down in some way, or letting him
down, although he deserved every minute of it." She
told Therese everything that had happened, especially
on the night the child was christened.

"You're very private really," Therese said. "How
long are you here now and you never told me that?"

"You never asked. I suppose we're both very private
in our own ways." Bridie shrugged her shoulders. "I

think that's what I meant earlier, about saying too much, exposing yourself. Maybe I shouldn't have told you now either, but I felt as if the ice had been broken a bit between us tonight."

"I'm hardly going to tell anybody."

"People can bring things up, to hurt somebody, if they're angry."

"Don't worry on that score. I know all about hurt."

"You do... Sure you have it made."

"Little do you know."

"Do you want to tell me?"

"I'll tell you, Bridie, when I'm ready." Therese looked her in the eyes and Bridie knew that she would. They sat silently for a long time in front of the flickering images on the television set, their minds far away.

"I wonder will he come back." It was Bridie who broke the spell.

"Who?" Therese was miles away.

"John. My husband."

"I'm glad you've told me what he's like in case he ever does come back. If he ever comes around here and tries something on he'll have me to deal with." Therese took the poker from beside the fire.

Bridie laughed at her. "Fuck him anyway," she said, "he really made a shite of my life." A tear rolled slowly from her right eye and down her face. Therese took her hand, but Bridie took it away quickly, wiped her face. "I haven't seen him for nearly two years and he's still able to upset me."

"Would you like a night-cap?" Not knowing what to say, Therese decided to do something practical. They sat quietly for a long while, looking into the fire, sipping their drinks. After some time Bridie told Therese not to be waiting up, she knew she had an early start in the morning.

"Will you be all right?"

"Don't worry about me." Bridie sat for in front of the fire, the television talking to itself in the corner. She'd felt safe as long as John was in prison, but she was beginning to worry now that his term was almost up. "Needless worry," she told herself, but that did little to ease the apprehension of the night. Two years had seemed such a long time when he was sentenced. She'd thought he'd never bother her again. The very thought of him being free bothered her now.

She'd never gone to see him in prison. She couldn't have faced him, wanted to forget all about him, start a new life for herself and her child. She'd left London as quickly as she could. Therese's small ad in the *Connacht Tribune* had been a life-saver. She hadn't thought she'd a chance of the job when she'd arrived for the interview with babe in arms. He had turned out to be her biggest advantage. Therese fell in love with Caomhán on the spot.

She hadn't realised how much she'd missed home until she came back to Ireland. Her family lived less than ten miles away, close to the coast road. Their house faced out across Galway Bay towards the Aran Islands. Bridie brought Caomhán to see them every week; the grandfather and grandmother were mad about the little fellow. The support of her family meant a lot to her but she wouldn't like to be under their feet either. She didn't have a place of her own yet, but that day would come, she promised herself. She'd be completely independent yet.

She remembered the first time she'd seen John, a big handsome red-haired man playing full-forward for the Naomh Eoin club in the inter-parish Gaelic football competition. He was on holiday from England at the time and he'd been his team's trump card, selling dummies to the local full-back with ease, and nonchalantly popping the ball over the bar. He had scored a goal and four points from play on a full-back who had got a trial for the Galway senior team. The crowd thought he was sensational.

He'd been introduced to Bridie that night at the dance in the marquee. She thought he was the most handsome man she ever met, tall and gracious, and such a good dancer. She had some doubts about letting him leave her home. "Don't worry," he'd said with a smile, "we'll have a chaperone." He told her a neighbour was with him. The man was a little simple, he said, but loved being seen with John in the Mercedes. "I can't go home without him," he'd laughed.

It was a clear summer night. John had driven down to the beach to see the "moon dancing on the water." It was all so romantic that she had thought his phrase poetic. They walked barefoot on the beach. It was heaven when he kissed her, and soon their tongues were intertwining. She was careful not to let him go too far, but this turned out to be far different from stopping one of the lads at the youth club from pawing her. But she was in the big league now and this was probably to be expected. It was just a matter of being firm, she thought.

His hands were all over her. She told him to stop but he wouldn't. He told her she wanted him as much as he wanted her. Micilín, his mate, seemed to have disappeared. As John slid his hand up her bare leg beneath her dress, Bridie pressed herself to him, as if she was going to give in to him. She kissed him, licked his ear, then whispered, "That's enough." She managed to get away from him and ran back to the car.

Bridie sat in the back seat of the Mercedes and locked both doors. Although the night was balmy she felt cold and apprehensive. John walked back slowly, sat into the driver's seat, lit a cigarette, and opened the window beside him to let out the smoke. He sat in silence for some time.

"It's past time for me to be at home," Bridie had said.

"You're some prick teaser."

"What?"

"You want it as badly as I do, but you're just playing hard to get."

"I want to go home."

"You don't know what's good for you."

"Just take me home, please."

"Let's go." Bridie was relieved when he started the car. John put a country and western tape in the stereo. A woman was singing *Lay the blanket on the ground*. The car moved off in a flurry of sand, but instead of heading for home John started to do handbrake turns on the strand. Bridie was filled with terror although there was no danger of crashing into anything on the beach. She thought of opening the door and rolling out, but the way the car was spinning in circles she'd surely be killed. He braked to a sudden stop, singing along with the country singer.

"Who needs a blanket when you have real leather upholstery?" He'd jumped across the back of the front seats, then he forced her to kiss him although she had kept her teeth clenched. "I know well that you have the hots for me. You're just a bit shy but you don't know what you're missing. They don't call me 'Big

John' for nothing." He slapped her face when she scraped his hand as he tore off her knickers. "Don't do that," he warned. There was no stopping him then.

John had blown the horn of the car when he was finished with her and his mate returned. The two men sat in the front smoking as she'd lain curled on the hard leather of the back seat. Micilín had leaned back after a while. "Any chance of you?" he asked. John hit him viciously with the back of his left hand across the face. "She's my woman," he said as he dumped his neighbour out of the car and drove off at speed. He talked about the match on the way home, about his hopes of getting on the county team, talked as if nothing had happened. She'd cried silently and bitterly on the back seat. Was this love?

It was the first time in years that Bridie had allowed that night's happenings through her mind. She was afraid to think any more about him, but knew she wouldn't sleep until that spool of hurt had run to its conclusion. It was as if a dam had burst when she talked to Therese, and there was no holding back the surge of memory and emotion. There was no way she would rest until she thought it all through. She'd sleep tomorrow, she promised herself, when Caomhán went for his afternoon rest.

Bridie readied a strong cup of coffee for herself, put more turf on the fire and sat remembering. John had come to their house the following Sunday. She could still see her father sitting close to the television, watching a match in his near-sighted way. John had walked in and asked, "Is Bridie going back to the currach racing in Carraroe?" What was she to do? Say this man had taken advantage of her the other night?

She knew now that it was rape but at that stage

she was just a vulnerable inexperienced seventeen-year-old. Who would have been blamed but herself for being such an *óinseach*? For allowing herself to be in such a position. She'd been reluctant to go with him, but her father had brooked no refusal. Footballers were all heroes to him. "Off with you," he had said, "the two of you might win the doubles currach race."

John was charm itself that day, and despite herself Bridie found she was enjoying the festival. It was a beautiful day with thousands congregated at the Coral strand. She began to feel, as she walked beside this handsome man, that what had happened the other night was what she should expect from a man. Maybe she was too stuffy, caught up in all this Christian doctrine stuff of keeping your virginity for the man you were to marry. What did the nuns know about it anyway? And the thought had struck her. Maybe they would marry.

They had gone from one pub to another on their way back from the festival. They went to a dance after closing time. John told her that he loved her. That was why he hadn't been able to restrain himself the last time. Bridie gave herself to him willingly that night, and many times more during the couple of months he spent at home. The passion and the pleasure made her feel she was living a dream. This was what it was like to be a grown woman. She forgot all about her Leaving Cert when he asked her to join him in London.

She'd already missed a period but she didn't care. They got their pre-nuptial papers filled before they left and married in Cricklewood. John drunkenly boasted on their wedding night that he'd put two other girls "up the pole." But he wouldn't have married anyone but Bridie. She didn't know whether to take him seriously or not.

They had a two-roomed bedsitter and kitchen upstairs in a house in Cricklewood Lane, near the Catholic church. Bridie tried hard to make a home of their cramped living quarters but she was lonely there. John left for work at seven in the morning. He didn't come back till midnight when he was drinking.

Bridie felt now, if anything, he worked too hard, earning a lot on overtime. This made him think that he deserved his "sessions" as he called his drinking bouts. Bridie longed to take a job, but he wouldn't allow her "in case anything happens to the baby." He forgot about the same baby when he punched her around the flat. How had Caomhán survived at all?

John seemed like a completely different man at times like that. It didn't happen every week or every month, but the danger was always there. He'd be very loving and helpful in the flat much of the time. They'd spend days together touring the city on the tube or sometimes in open-topped buses, very much in love. He'd promise never to drink again, and he'd make a genuine effort to keep that promise. All would be forgiven. Then the tension would slowly build up inside him like a bomb primed to explode.

It often seemed that he didn't remember what he had done the previous night. It was only when he saw that he'd beaten her black and blue or broken up the furniture that he seemed to realise the enormity of what he had done. He'd cry like a child, melting her heart with his tears. And then she'd kiss him with her bruised lips and the whole love-hate cycle would start again.

Bridie reminded herself again that not everything about her time in London had been bad, even though it all seemed like a nightmare now. John was never mean and she had plenty of ready money on hand to go and explore the city, often taking a tube train from one end to the other, surfacing from time to time to window-shop. She'd felt since that she learned more from art galleries and libraries than she'd have learned if she'd stayed on at school for her Leaving Certificate.

Some days she just wandered around Cricklewood itself. She found it a much pleasanter place than the way people talked about it back at home in Connemara. There was a place near the local church where ducks and geese wandered around a kind of yard cum garden, just as you'd see them at home. Three days before her eighteenth birthday she'd given birth to Caomhán without complications or very much pain. The doctor had told her she was the picture of good health.

For a wonderful month Bridie thought John had changed completely from the moment he'd taken his son in his arms. She could still see the tiny baby in the big strong hands and the wonder in the grown man's eyes at the helplessness and perfection of the child. He'd taken a drink to celebrate the baptism He got cantankerous when their friends had left. He'd said the baby wasn't his. He called her "bitch," and "whore." When she didn't reply he had belted her. He kicked her out the door, down the stairs...

She'd been lucky to be still in hospital when his court case came up. She couldn't have brought herself to give evidence against him. The assault and battery charge was pushed through by police witnesses, especially the doctor and social worker who treated her. There was also his own half-hearted admission. Or maybe he really didn't remember, as the social worker suggested. She thought he probably believed she informed on him, although she'd nothing at all to do with the court case.

What would she do if he came back? Would he be able to work the same old magic, persuade her he had changed? Maybe he wouldn't come near her at all, maybe shame would keep him from showing his face after a couple of years in prison. She doubted it. Shame was not a word you'd associate with John. "One thing sure," she told herself, "there is no way he's taking Caomhán from me."

It was Caomhán who woke her in the middle of the night, where she'd fallen asleep on the couch. She woke up to find the big blue eyes looking at her, his bottle hanging by the teat from his mouth. He'd climbed from his cot when he woke up, uncomfortable in his wet nappy. She changed him and took him into her bed, hoping he wouldn't wake too early in the morning.

Therese was in high good humour at the breakfast table. Bridie was hardly able to keep her eyes open. Thatch was to spend the day flying by helicopter from one factory to another in the Mayo and Donegal Gaeltachts, Tourmakeady, Belmullet, Gweedore, and on to Tory Island. She'd stop at Killybegs on the return journey to meet fishermen from Aran and Connemara who were based there. She was trying to persuade them to relocate their boats in Rossaveal on the Connemara coast so that their families would strengthen the local communities, especially the island ones.

"Maybe you'd like to go for a drink with me tonight, Bridie?"

"How can I? What about Caomhán?"

"There is such a thing as a baby-sitter. I'll pay if you

want."

"I'm well able to pay my own bills, thank you."

"You weren't out for a long time."

"I was back at home the other day."

"A night out I'm talking about. A young girl like you. You need to get out with the crowd. There'll be a good session tonight."

"I'll try to get someone, but I don't like to be long away from him."

"You have to have a break from him now and again. He'll get on your nerves if you're with him all the time. You'll feel a lot better tomorrow."

"I'm bad enough as I am, without having a hangover as well."

"It's up to yourself, Bridie. I won't force you. We'll be time enough going out at half past nine."

"I'll think about it."

"Don't just think, do," Therese repeated one of her mottoes before leaving. Bridie told herself Thatch was right. A break would be good for her. She'd ask Susan, her sister, to come over on the bus and spend the night with Caomhán. At fifteen, Susan would be delighted with the pocket money as well as the chance to mother her nephew.

It was only when she began to think about what she'd wear that Bridie realised how long it was since she'd been out anywhere apart from the shop, or to the church or to see her parents. She spent the day wondering what she'd do with her hair, what she'd wear. It was like being a teenager again, she thought, enjoying the apprehension.

Would she wear the high leather boots or just a pair of runners? She had the boots a couple of years and they were probably out of fashion. So what? She didn't care what anyone thought. Anyway what would be more casual than a session in a pub? Would she stand out like a sore thumb among all the young ones with factory or secretarial jobs? She spent any money she had on Caomhán rather than on herself. What about the denim skirt and the blue jumper? Would she even fit into the skirt?

Why did she think everyone would be looking at her? she asked herself. Places like that were usually so dark you could hardly see your drink. She envied Therese her self-confidence, her ability to mix with high and low, rich and poor, to be at ease with everyone. But wouldn't she be all right when she was with her? Therese would keep the conversation going, whoever they met.

"Am I out of my mind?" she asked her image in the mirror. "You'd think you were a young one out on her first date. What is there to it but drink and music and cigarette smoke?" Suppose some high-up manager friend of Therese asked her a question. What do people like that talk about? Current affairs. She made a mental note to listen to the news. Then she laughed at herself again. "What do people in pubs talk, except *seafóid*?" It would be good to be out again among the crowd. It was as if a couple of years of her life had been stolen from her.

❧

Long before the day he left prison, John had made up his mind never to spend a day in a place like that again. The surest way to do that was to stay off the drink. Bridie had been right all along, he thought, although he hadn't heeded her at the time. Drink lay at the root of his troubles. As far as he could make out many of the young men who shared the prison yard and recreation halls with him would never have been there either only for drink, drugs and the crime needed to feed their habits.

Many of them managed to feed the same habits while inside. There were always ways and means of smuggling stuff, especially to those who were part of a gang or had taken a rap to save a boss's bacon. Most of them ended up losing their good conduct remission and that was something John had been careful to avoid. A year and a half had been long enough, too long for an Irishman in an English jail.

There had been some racist taunts in the beginning, a bit of aggro now and again when there was a bomb in London or a couple of soldiers were killed in Northern Ireland. Some of the blokes had been in the army and felt it might have been them. As time went on and fellows had got to know each other a kind of camaraderie had developed. There were Irish jokes, in bad taste but in good fun. Many of his fellow inmates had been on the fringes of society much as he'd been. And they hated authority and screws far more.

John had managed to give the impression that there had been some kind of miscarriage of justice in his case. There was still a lot of sympathy for the Birmingham Six, the Maguires, the Guildford Four, Judith Ward, all of whose convictions were later overturned. He had turned his Irishness into a badge of honour as if he was more sinned against than sinning. While others bragged about their crimes, he acted the wounded innocent. By the time he got out he almost believed it himself as the blokes inside did. They made "Paddy" a kind of a hero. He had a lump in his throat the day he said goodbye.

John had been furious with his wife when he was first locked up but he'd gradually come to understand and see her point of view. It had taken him a long time to face the fact that he'd beaten her black and blue. He had thrown his own wife, the woman he loved, the mother of his child, down the stairs and gone back to bed. There were no excuses for behaviour like that. He wanted now more than anything to make everything up to Bridie, but she'd want to have nothing to do with him. And who could blame her?

He'd served his time, paid his debt to society. He was young, most of his life still in front of him. It was all about learning from your mistakes. "How many of the saints made a bollocks of their lives," he asked himself, "and then ended up in the heights of Heaven?" St Peter was definitely one. Denied Our Lord and was handed the keys of the kingdom a few weeks later. And Thomas poking around Jesus' wounds with his fingers to make sure it was him that was in it. John had never done anything remotely as bad as either of them, he told himself. Most men hit the wife a few skelps now and again.

That wasn't to say that it was right, but women could be right bitches sometimes, get on your nerves nagging and complaining if you weren't home in time, didn't bring them flowers, didn't pay them compliments. What they fancied one day didn't work at all another day. Unpredictable. That was the word for it. Always have you on your toes, and when you bent over backwards trying to please them, it would turn out that it was something else altogether they were looking for. That was fine if you were sober, but when a man had done a bit of a tear after a hard day's work and came home to find that there was no dinner...

The very same kind of thing had annoyed his father before him. John remembered the time he came back from the cattle mart well oiled late at night. He'd got the highest price paid out the same day and naturally enough had celebrated on the way home. His wife was in bed, his dinner in cinders. He had taken his belt to her as he would to one of the children. He remembered how he and his brothers huddled in bed as they listened to the screams and the crack of the leather. His mother got up and boiled him a feed of potatoes in the middle of the night.

The children had thought their parents would never speak to each other again after that. As it turned out they hadn't got up the next day until midday and were all lovey dovey for days afterwards. His father had bought his mother a new dress the following Saturday. There was no talk that time of sending for the guards, no talk of a woman leaving home and making a new life for herself.

"It's hard to live with them, but you can't live without them," John told himself. A lot could be forgiven when a woman turned to you in the middle of the night hot and clammy, her nightie slipping up around her waist, her lips moist and kissable, her tongue darting like a snake's fang. That was the best ride of all, the unexpected, the unpredictable. At times like that you didn't mind at all if a woman was unpredictable, riding you like a pony one night, writhing beneath you the next, giving you a blow-job the night she was afraid of getting pregnant. "It's been too long," he sighed.

He'd do his best to get them back. After all she was

still his wife, the mother of his child. With God's help they might be able to get together again, learn from past mistakes and take it from there. Things might work out better if they were back at home in Ireland, their families near them. A man didn't realise it when he was young, but there was a lot to be said for the Irish way of doing things, having grannies and granddads around when children were growing up. It took a lot of the pressure off parents.

He knew that Bridie and the child had gone back. It was not that she wrote to tell him. But then he'd never tried to write to her either. His mates had visited him for a while after he was put in first, but their visits fell off gradually as some went back home, others followed the building companies to European sites. They had to go where the work was when the arse fell out of the British economy. The rest just lost interest. They had nothing to talk about when they were not in pubs.

The only visitor he had for the last year was his mother. She was in Birmingham for her sister's funeral and came down to see him. He hadn't enjoyed her visit. She'd cried all the time, partly for her sister; they'd been close. It was the shame that had really got to her, and the prison, although she'd only seen the best of it, the visitors' meeting room. "Why did you ever marry that strap?" she'd asked, blaming everything on Bridie. "Isn't it many's the belt I got from your father, and I didn't go snivelling to the guards."

John felt proud that he didn't waste his time inside. He buckled down to work, learning a lot about woodwork and metalwork, honing the skills he'd learned at the vocational school and the Government training course back at home. He'd always been good with his hands, and looked forward to building a house for Bridie and himself and their family. His mother had promised a site on their own land, "when you get your act together."

Through the good offices of the prison probation scheme he had got a small room in Camden Town. "They must think that every Paddy is at home in the Town," he'd laughed to himself as the well-meaning officer showed him where he would be staying. He'd only wait as long as he had to. The terms of his probation meant that he had to do a transition course to prepare him for life on the outside. He felt the course was a waste of time. The bloke in charge hadn't much interest. He was sure that John would be "inside again within the year, just like the rest of them."

He'd be finished with that before Christmas so he'd be back yonder in time for the turkey. The sooner the better. He could see the heathery hills in his mind's eye, patches of green here and there, little fields wrested from the blanket bog to grow potatoes, oats, vegetables. A couple of scarce trees bent by the wind, the great expanse of the ocean. Home. It would be hard in the beginning to face neighbours who thought prison the ultimate disgrace. So what? They all had skeletons in their own cupboards. Fuck them. They'd soon think of someone else to talk about.

He still loved Bridie. John had no doubt now about that. Had ever a day passed in the prison that he hadn't thought about her? The way she walked, threw her long hair back over her shoulder, how handsome she was in a brooding sort of way. Hadn't she forgiven him time and time again, taken him back, tried again? Until the night the child was baptised and things had gone too far...

Whatever had come over him? Drink. That's what had come over him. Whiskey. In a way he was lucky that it wasn't a life sentence he was putting in for her murder. It had come as a shock to him when the police had told him how badly he had battered Bridie. It frightened him to think he could lose control to that extent, not even remember what had happened. "Well, that was then, this is now." He was pleased to find himself with such a positive attitude to life. "Once I stay away from the drink..."

He intended to stay at home after Christmas, never to set foot in England again. Life was more natural back West, he thought. A man would be better off on the dole there. Better poor back home than fed up on a good income in London. The Big Smoke was fine when you were young, footloose and fancy-free as they used to say, trying to escape the claustrophobia of home and Church and Irish society to sow some wild oats.

He had sown a fair bit of wild oats in his time, he remembered, and in a fair few different fields. He'd been a shy enough seventeen-year-old when he came over to London. He'd never even had sex. That was soon remedied, ten pounds from his first pay-packet. He had bungled his first attempt, coming in a condom in the girl's hand as she tried to direct him to his destination. Fair play to her, she'd given him value for his money, caressed him until he was ready again, allowed him a second go, told him it was worth it as she seldom got virgins, and never had a "Paddyvirgin" before.

He had never failed again after that. Soon enough he was getting for nothing what he had paid for in the beginning. But it was money well spent, an investment almost. He'd learned skills that he was never going to forget. It was a lot safer with young girls of course, a lot less danger of disease. He met Irish girls at dances, lonely and away from home, delighted to hear someone who could speak the language, even if they didn't have two words of it to rub together themselves.

It wasn't that he just wanted to take advantage of them. Bridie had often accused him of that. She hated to think that he had a life before he met her. She couldn't understand that all that was in the past. In fact he'd never been with anyone else since they'd met three years before. He'd liked the other girls and thought about marrying nearly every one of them he'd been with at one time or another. Not the ones on the game, of course, you had to draw the line somewhere. As for taking advantage, if anything some of them took advantage of him because he was good-looking, athletic, a good footballer.

He'd play football again for the local club. He'd missed that a lot. They used to play soccer in the prison yard, and he'd learned a few skills from the Cockneys that he could put to good use in Gaelic football. Although he'd enjoyed the games more than anything else inside, soccer never thrilled him like Gaelic, the way he used to rise to meet a high ball, round a player or two with a couple of deft dummies and pop the ball over the bar or sink it in the net. He hoped his son would have the same skill.

He wondered how the young fellow was. He would be walking now, talking maybe. Wouldn't it be nice to be called "Daddy." She'd have to let him have access to his son, whatever about coming to live with him. That was the law. He was sure of it. But Bridie wouldn't mind. She was a good girl at the back of it all. "May he be the first of many," he said to himself.

It amazed John that he could have forgotten the name of his own son. But then he hadn't been baptised until the day his troubles started, and they'd never called him anything except "the baby" until then. What was that name she had come up with? Something Irish. He remembered the priest had difficulty pronouncing it. Some saint the fishermen in Galway Bay had a devotion to. He thought of Mac Duach and Mac Dara, but he knew it wasn't one of them, something beginning with a "C" or was it an "S"? He'd know soon enough.

He'd send him money for Christmas. The lads had sold the Mercedes for him when he was convicted. The money was lying in a bank account he didn't intend to touch until he was going home. Apart from the present for the young fellow. That would help to soften Bridie's cough. Long ago he should have thought of it, but better late than never. Bridie would come around all right.

He remembered how he'd never thought of her as anything but "the bitch" when he went to prison first, but that changed with time. He'd come to realise that the fault was all his own. Well, not his fault really, he told himself, but the drink. "Cut that out and you'll be all right. I can't wait to see her; and what the hell was it that she called the young fellow again?"

❧

Therese was late. Bridie worried that something might have happened the helicopter that was to take her around on her inspection. Susan had come on the bus after school and taken Caomhán for a walk while

Bridie tidied and vacuumed the house for the second time that day. Bridie let a shout at Caomhán when he arrived back with his aunt, muck on his shoes.

"What's wrong with you?" Susan asked. "You must be afraid of your life of that old Thatch, or whatever it is they call her."

"Therese is her name, and I'm fed up scrubbing and cleaning since morning." Bridie sat down suddenly on an armchair, dropping the cleaning materials beside her. Then she burst out laughing.

"Are you gone crazy or something?"

"I've just remembered an old joke."

"Tell us."

"It might be too crude for your little ears," she mocked her young sister.

"Will you give over, woman."

"It's just about a nun that went up to the Reverend Mother one day and complained: 'There's nothing going on around here except fucking and scrubbing,' she said, 'and I'm doing all the scrubbing'." She knew Susan would enjoy that. There were nuns in her own school. "Well, that's what I feel," Bridie said. "I'm just a fucking scrubber."

"Did you hear the one," Susan asked conspiratorially, "about the nun that went to confession and told the priest that a man had put his hand on her knee. For her penance he told her to go and dip her knee in the holy water font." Susan giggled. "When she got there the Reverend Mother was sitting in the font."

"Yeah," Bridie said, absentmindedly.

"Ah, you're as dry. What's wrong with you?" Susan had taken off the child's shoes and socks and he was running about in his bare feet.

"Oh, I don't know, the time of the month maybe. I'm full of tension. You know yourself. Sorry." She held out her arms to Caomhán. "Lovey for Mammy." He put his arms around her neck and hugged. "Mammy sorry for shouting." She broke her own rules about not using baby talk.

"Isn't this a grand soft life too," Susan was looking around, "nothing to do but look after this place, prepare a few meals, all the mod cons. I can't wait to finish that frigging school and be my own boss for a change."

"Finish school if you have any sense. I can tell you that there's nothing glamorous about this. This is about as dead end a job as you can get. I wouldn't be doing it except that it suits Caomhán until he gets on his feet."

"Old Thatch isn't that bad, is she?"

"If she hears you calling her that," Bridie laughed, "especially the old bit! But I'd prefer to be working for myself than be anyone's skivvy."

"Why don't you have another baby? You'd have enough of an allowance not to have to work."

"That's the most stupid thing I ever heard. That kind of talk really gets up my hole." Bridie liked to use the kind of teenage language her sister used. "I hear people on radio programmes every second day accusing girls of having babies for the sake of the money. If the people talking had to live on the money they get... Anyway I hope you won't be as silly as your sister."

"I'd prefer anything to that stupid school. It's so boring." Susan stretched out the word boring to its limit.

"If it's boring you want, girl, try housework for

size," Bridie said; "it's never done and there's no thanks for it."

"Isn't it worth it for this doteen."

"That's the very same thing Therese calls him, doteen. You'd think he was her own half the time." Bridie looked at her watch. "Where the hell is she? It's just like something that'd happen. When I have everything ready and a baby-sitter got, she doesn't turn up at all. All dressed up and nowhere to go."

"Something might have turned up at work."

"Something might have turned up all right." She held a finger out in front of her in a phallic gesture. "The way that one flirts with the men, I wouldn't be surprised what might turn up. I wouldn't put anything past her."

"Bridie!" Susan feigned shock.

"Maybe that's how she attracts the jobs." Bridie shook with laughter. "Oh, God forgive me."

"There's great crack in you all of a sudden, for someone that was so cranky a while ago." Susan was enjoying the fact that her sister was treating her as an equal rather than as a little girl, as her parents did.

"I suppose that I take life too seriously most of the time," Bridie said, standing up and swirling around, "but I'm breaking out tonight. If that one comes. I don't know why I'm so nervous."

"I don't either, an ould wan like you," Susan joked. Bridie lifted her fist in mock anger.

It was nearly nine o'clock when Therese breezed into the house, sending shoes and clothes flying in all directions. She had to take the helicopter pilot for a meal, she said. "Sorry, I'll be ready in ten minutes. We'll still be there before there's too much of a crowd."

Susan skitted with laughter when Therese emerged naked from the bathroom and went to her own room. "Have a bit of manners," Bridie said to her, "you'd think you never saw a woman before."

"I never saw one as thin as that. I thought she was a boy."

"Then you never saw a boy either."

"Maybe I did. Maybe I didn't."

"Tell me more."

"We do have a little brother at home."

"No need to act so innocent." The sisters continued to joke with each other until Therese was ready, true to her word, at twenty past nine.

Bridie was not as nervous as she expected to be as they entered the pub. The place was nearly full. All the attention turned to Therese as she entered. "Hi, Thatch," workmen called. Civil servants from the Gaeltacht Board were more discreet but nonetheless welcoming. There were offers of drinks, stools to sit on, a great sense of enjoyment and well-being.

The whole area had taken on new life in the last few years; whole families had moved home from the United States and Britain since work became available. It was as if the seventies had come back, plenty of work, plenty of money, plenty of fun, people no longer depended on tourists to fill pubs. "Winter is as good as summer," some of the old people had a habit of saying, "and every day is a Christmas."

Therese ordered two gin and tonics. Bridie was slightly annoyed that she wasn't asked what she wanted but then that was what she would have ordered anyway. Therese put the glass and the little bottle into her hands and then she excused herself and began to move around, greeting everyone by name. A bee to the flowers, Bridie thought, wondering who was sucking whose honey.

Bridie wasn't long standing on her own. She got a kiss on the cheek, and then a hug from Peadar Halloran who had been in her class at the community school. "Don't tell me it's yourself," he enthused.

"I think it is," she laughed, "and how are you? Long time no see."

"You'll have another?" He indicated her drink, and before she'd time to reply he was gone to the counter for another one.

"Are you still in the RTC?" she asked when he came back. She was surprised that a student would be so flush with money.

"Still there, but I spent the summer in Chicago, and my tax came back today so tonight's the night, as they say."

"What are you doing in college?"

"Business studies, more business than study, if you get me. With a bit of luck I'll be qualified in the summer."

"What then?"

"I have an idea for a little industry, if I can knock the money out of your friend Thatch there."

"That explains why you came talking to me," Bridie teased him, "looking for the inside information."

"You know well I always fancied you."

"You did not."

"We used to have great ould crack at the school long ago."

"Long ago. It's not more than three years yet."

"You know what I mean. Do you remember that time we went up to Dublin for the debates? The two of us went to the pictures, the poor nun going crackers around O'Connell Street searching for us."

"I remember the shock I got," Bridie laughed, "when I saw her coming towards us outside the GPO between two big giants of guards. I thought that she'd been arrested for something."

"The guards had an awful job trying to cool her down."

"No wonder we were never brought to another debate."

"It's not that we weren't good, even if I say so myself. You were the best speaker I ever heard in a debate. We'd probably have won the All-Ireland if we hadn't been grounded for that episode at the pictures." As Peadar complimented her, Bridie thought of how quickly her self-confidence had ebbed away.

"It feels like another life altogether," she said.

"Do you know that you broke my heart when you married that fellow." His comment surprised Bridie.

"You're joking me. Sure we weren't going out together, or anything."

"But we went everywhere together, the youth club, the debates, we were on the same team in the junior currach races. I thought it was only a matter of time. I can tell you that I had my cap set at you. In my own mind, anyway. And you're as beautiful as ever." Bridie wondered how much he'd drunk.

"Flattery will get you nowhere," she said, enjoying the compliments at the same time; "give over your old *plámás*."

"It's no *plámás* at all. You're as fine a bit of stuff as is in here tonight." He surveyed the bar. "You're ten times better looking than that Thatch, although all the fellows are killed talking about her."

"Don't let her hear you," Bridie quipped, "sure

she's like a model."

"Skin and bone," Peadar said. "I like to see a woman with a bit of lining, a bit of stuffing, not like a bag of bones."

"Too much upholstery some of us have," Bridie observed. She'd found it hard to squeeze into the denim skirt.

"Don't knock yourself," her old schoolmate said, a glazed kind of look in his eyes. "If you don't mind now, I have to see a man about a dog. We'll talk again." Bridie wondered again about his drinking. He seemed completely in control most of the time. But she remembered John's drinking bouts all too well. She knew a person can be coherent one minute and in a drunken stupor the next.

"It's my turn. I'm able to buy a drink as well as the next person," she said, when Therese arrived back with more drink.

"Take it easy, keep your knickers on," Therese said. "These come from the workmen in the corner. Don't insult them by refusing."

"I'd hate to insult anyone," Bridie smiled. She knew she was inclined to get paranoid too quickly about such things. Did she need to show her independence by such a silly thing as buying a round of drink. Susan was right, she did need to ease up. She was still determined to buy the next round though.

The music started at last. Between that and the fact that the drink seemed to relax her, Bridie began to enjoy the night. The music was so loud that conversation was impossible. She liked that. It gave her an opportunity to stand back from everything and everybody, observe, allow the nerves and worry of the last few years to fall away from her like an old coat.

The heavy rock changed to *céilí*. Inhibitions disappeared in a couple of wild "yahoos." Thatch was out in all the sets. She was as good a dancer as there was in the pub. "Why wouldn't she be?" Bridie thought, "she gets plenty of practice anyway, out nearly every night." Still, she could only admire her freedom of spirit as well as movement. "The freest person I ever saw," thought Bridie. Her friend's attitude seemed to be, "To hell with what anyone thinks, as long as I'm doing my job to the best of my ability."

Peadar Halloran grabbed Bridie's hand and with a wild exuberant yell led her out for the next set. The steps came back as if she'd danced yesterday. Between the drink and the swings she had a reel in her head when it finished. From then until closing time Bridie forgot about herself, let herself go, enjoyed herself so much that she regretted that the night had to come to an end.

"Well, that wasn't too bad." Therese poured them each a drink when they got home. Susan had obviously gone to bed some time before because the fire had nearly gone out. When she'd checked on Caomhán, Bridie lit the fire again with a fire-lighter and a few sticks. They sat deep in the big easy chairs, tired and relaxed, the music of the night still ringing in their ears.

"I'm as drunk as a lord," Bridie said, "and sure Caomhán will be up in no time."

"Relax, for God's sake. Won't Susan see to him until we get up. That little fellow twists you around his little finger. You have to live too."

"Just as well he's no longer breast-feeding, or he'd have a hangover as bad as myself in the morning."

"It wouldn't do him one bit of harm," Therese

stretched and yawned contentedly, "any more than yourself."

"Thanks for taking me out tonight, Therese. You were right all along. I need to get out a bit oftener."

"I thought you'd be mad with me for not staying with you all the time, but I have to keep that crowd with me."

"I understand that. Sure I was all right on my own."

"Howdo on your own," Therese joked, "you didn't introduce me to the fine thing."

"Fine thing? Oh, you mean Peadar Halloran? He was in the same class as me at the secondary school."

"He'd be a bit young for me so," Therese said.

"He'll soon be going to see you about some new project. He's studying business in the RTC."

"He fairly studied your own business tonight. He spent his time staring down your cleavage."

"He did not, and anyway I haven't any bosom in this thing." Bridie straightened up her top. "Lots of booze-um, though."

Therese ignored her joke. "Sure I was watching him all night."

"Isn't it little you had to do?"

"Not much passes unknown to me."

"You would think it's jealous you are."

"If I had a pair like that, I wouldn't be left on the shelf the way I am," Therese laughed.

"You're not on any shelf. You could have your choice of men."

"Oh, yes."

"Even Peadar was fancying you tonight."

"I gave up baby snatching a long time ago."

"Well, what about the older, more mature type?"

"Old fogies like myself, you mean?"

"You could have anyone you want."

"No more than yourself, Bridie, I've had enough of them."

"But you were never married to one of them like I was?"

"I was fed up with men long before I was marriage age."

"You were, like... You're the biggest flirt I ever saw."

"Well, as I said before, you don't see me letting any of them get too close."

"Still waiting for the right one to come along," Bridie said airily. Therese's next question came as a bit of a shock to her. "Did your father ever abuse you?"

"Sure he never stops giving out, but there's no harm in him."

"Don't be dumb, you know well what I mean."

Bridie suddenly understood. "Your own father? He couldn't."

"He did."

"I'm sorry." Bridie didn't know what to say.

"Don't be sorry. It wasn't your fault."

"I know, but I can imagine..."

"From the time I was about five until I went to boarding school." Therese gulped a little as if she was finding it hard to talk. "I never met many people that actually enjoyed boarding school. But I did. It was the best thing that ever happened to me. Because it got me away from him."

"What about your mother?"

"She couldn't be without knowing about it. She certainly didn't do anything. Unless it was her idea to send me to boarding school."

"Didn't you tell her?"

"Sex was a dirty word in our house. It was something

that wasn't supposed to exist. It'd be impossible for me to talk to my mother about anything like that. She was a woman of the old school. A devout Irish Catholic mother. I remember when I had my period the first time. I thought my father had injured me. Only for the other girls at school..."

"I don't believe that my father would even think of doing anything like that." Suddenly Bridie began to laugh uncontrollably. "I'm awful sorry," she said when she managed to stop, "you'll think I'm terrible."

"What were you thinking about?" Therese smiled to ease her embarrassment. She knew Bridie felt ashamed about her sudden outburst of awkward laughter.

"I often used to wonder if my father even knew how to do it with my mother. He was over fifty when they got married, a lot older than she was."

"The poor man." Therese really enjoyed the company of Bridie's father when they went back with Caomhán to visit her parents. "He's not that innocent, he hasn't that gamey eye for nothing."

"It must have been terrible for you growing up," said Bridie thoughtfully.

"I almost took it for granted after a while. I used to think that it was part of every little girl's life, even though I knew in my heart and soul that it was wrong. It was only when I went to England that I realised how common child abuse is. And of course it began to come to light in this country around that time too."

"Your mother must have known." Bridie was thinking about her own mother, a woman that nothing much would happen unknown to, in the house or outside it.

"Don't worry... I've tried hard to see it from her

point of view." Therese shook her head. "I've heard of cases where a mother didn't realise what was going on. And if she did know what was she to do at the time? Complain? A woman could be committed to a psychiatric home for less, and I'm sure that many a one was. Or worse again, she'd be given the road. What would she live on? Where would she go? The men had all the power. Even more than they have now."

"I remember hearing about a case where the mother knew about it," Bridie said, "but she was too afraid of her husband to tell anyone."

"I can understand a case like that, where a man is a right brute. But my father was, still is the most respectable man in the parish, the local shopkeeper, the chairman of the Cumann, the head of the sodality, if they have sodalities any more."

"There was always a law in the land."

"What little girl is going to have her father dragged into court? The family dragged through the mud? Who'd have believed her anyway? They'd have put it down to a dirty mind, a filthy imagination. After all that's happened in the meantime, at least a girl might be listened to today, but twenty years ago..."

"Do you hate all men because of what he did to you?" Bridie put her hand over her glass to prevent Therese pouring her another drink, but she relented. She thought her friend needed an ear to listen, as Bridie had needed one the night before. She felt that they might talk more freely in drink.

"I like men," Therese replied. "I like every man who was in that bar tonight. I like them on a light everyday, social level. I understand in here," she put her hand to her head, "that every man is different. But after what

I went through I could never sleep with any of them. I'd be cold, frigid, an icicle."

"Did you ever try?" Bridie blushed when she thought of what she'd said. "Sorry, I have no right to ask that."

"You try anything once." Therese gave a nervous little laugh. "He thought that it was himself that wasn't up to it."

"Did you ever look for help?"

"A shrink? I wouldn't be able to go to a man anyway. I've often thought of ringing up the Rape Crisis Centre or something."

"Why don't you?"

"I'd be afraid of all that would be raked up, things I mightn't want to face. And they might want me to take him to court or something. I couldn't do that. Not at his age, not after this length of time. I don't even want to see him, let alone give evidence against him in court."

"But they might help you deal with it."

"I deal with it in my own way." Therese's reply was almost curt. "Most of the time I just ignore it, force myself to forget it. To be quite honest, you're the very first person I've ever told about it."

"Sure what can I do?" Bridie felt helpless.

"You listen. That's the important thing, and I don't think you're going to go around the place telling everybody."

"I haven't a notion."

"I know that. I know that even though you're a lot younger than me, you've suffered a lot in the past few years. You understand more than most. I hope I'm not landing you with a big burden. That you won't think less of me because of what I told you." Therese paused. "A lot of the time I don't know how any woman survives, and then I look at some of the women in the office and they don't seem to have a care in the world."

"I'm sure they think the same when they look at you. You're the envy of every woman west of the Corrib."

"The playgirl of the western world," Therese said, with a sarcastic snigger. "The plaything of the western world, that's what a woman is."

"I wonder does it go on in every society?"

"It seems to have been taboo in many of the cultures." Therese really only had a vague idea about it. "I hate using the word 'primitive'. Most of them were far more civilised than we are."

"You'd think," Bridie had got up to make two cups of coffee, "that Ireland is the tabooest country of them all."

"Like any kind of a law, a taboo can be a great protection, but it can be used as a cover-up just as easily if someone is cynical enough to use it. No one, but no one in their wildest dreams would suspect my father of child abuse. But he was able to hide behind the great taboo and get away with it."

"Some people say it's a disease, that people can't control themselves."

"Well, if they can't, somebody else should control them."

"I heard it argued in a court case about a priest or a Christian Brother, I don't know which, that it was some kind of an addiction, like drink or drugs."

"If that's the case the person with the addiction should be kept well away from children." Therese warmed to the subject. "I've always thought the Church's real argument against altar girls was never publicly expressed, that the reason they don't allow it is to keep girls out of the danger of being alone with a man in a sacristy. I don't agree with Rome on many things, but I would agree with them on that. In principle I'd be all in favour of equality of the sexes. In practice I'd be all in favour of protecting the innocent."

"You'll never forgive your father?"

Therese shrugged. "I hardly ever even think of him."

"I think of mine every day, of every member of the family, what they're doing, where they are at this very moment."

"Some people are born lucky."

"I suppose I was," Bridie mused, then laughed. "A pity it didn't last."

"But it did," her friend reminded her, "you have a stability I just long for."

"I have all right. A jailbird husband, a broken marriage, rearing a child on my own, a job as somebody's maid. That's stability for you."

"You're sound emotionally, Bridie."

"I'd prefer to be sound financially."

"You'll realise it some day. It really is a treasure of great price."

"I thought that it was between our legs we were supposed to have that." Bridie's eyes twinkled with laughter.

"What are you on about?" Therese smiled at her.

"The same as yourself, the treasure of great price."

"You mean the pleasure of great price. And what a price."

"God's gift to mankind."

"Typical God."

"Wasn't there some famous musician said that to a woman?"

"Go on."

"You know more about these things than I do."

"Not the dirty bits, I don't." Therese laughed.

"Sir John Barbarossa, or something."

"Barbirolli."

"You can call him Barbra Streisand for all I care. It doesn't matter. Anyway there was this girl trying to play the viola, or bass, some kind of a big fiddle anyway. And do you know what your man said?" Bridie tried to put on a posh English accent. "'There you are, madam, with God's gift to mankind between your legs, and all you can do is scratch it'."

"You could do worse."

"You're awful."

"It's you that's coming up with these weird and wonderful jokes."

"It drives men crazy, you know, women talking."

"It drives ourselves crazy too a lot of the time."

"Do you know what John used to call it? Twat-talk. He couldn't understand why I'd want to have a big long natter. And the funny thing is, they think that women talk about nothing, or about silly things. They never see the things that you don't say, or what someone means behind the lot of it."

"I'm often told that I think like a man."

"You mean that you have a one-track mind?" Bridie winked.

"I suppose it has something to do with business. You have to be able to play them at their own game, be as logical and tough and mean as they're supposed to be, and bring a woman's intuition to it at the same time."

"You can buy and sell most of them. You wouldn't be where you are, at the top of the pile, if you couldn't."

"The top of the heap," Therese joked, "the heap of shite."

"You'll meet the right man yet."

"I don't want to meet the right man. That's just what a man would say."

"Not all men are the same."

"Tell me where the good ones are."

"They must be there," Bridie laughed, "somewhere."

"When women really come to power, when we take over the world, we'll do away with them altogether."

"You'd still need the odd one to keep the next generation going."

"All you'd need is their seed. Once the sperm banks were full... They'd enjoy that part of it all right, making their deposits in the banks." Therese hadn't felt as drunk in a long time.

"In fairness to them all the same, they've more to offer than some kind of an injection. There's a bit of pleasure involved."

"We can provide that ourselves too. DIY. Self-service." Therese spluttered with laughter into her drink.

"I thought you meant women together."

"Nothing wrong with that either."

"It's worse you're getting," Bridie said.

"There's more to life..."

"Did you ever think of having a child outside marriage? You're really good with Caomhán."

"I've him spoiled on you."

"You'd make a very good mother."

"I don't think I'd have the patience. Things suit me as they are, Caomhán in the house, being able to give him whatever motherly love there is in me. But I couldn't do it all day every day. Someone like me has to make that choice, between a public and a private life. I made my choice a long time ago."

"Half the women of the world work now, and rear a family at the same time."

"Is it themselves that are rearing the family," Therese asked, "or their childminders? What I do like to see, and fair play to the men that do it, is fathers who stay at home to rear or help rear their children."

"You'd stay at home if you had children?"

"I'd be old-fashioned in that way, but then that question won't arise. I've made my choice. My job is my child, my pet, my passion."

"It's a pity I haven't a proper job," Bridie said regretfully. "We'd be on the same level then."

"Don't be trying to come down to my level." Therese tried to treat it lightly. She felt they'd discussed all that the night before. In some ways she felt that this was her night, and here was Bridie beginning to talk about herself again. "You have Caomhán," she said, "isn't that enough for you."

"When did you ever meet the person that had enough?" Bridie said muzzily. The room was beginning to spin, as her teeth began to water. She was going to be sick. She tried to stand, but felt weak. "I'll have to go to the bathroom..." The last thing she remembered was throwing up on the fine wool carpet. When she woke up in the middle of the night she was in Therese's bed. Therese's arm was around her. She slipped quietly out of bed and went to the kitchen for a drink of water.

She never remembered feeling so sick in her life. Her head was splitting. Her stomach felt as if it was on fire. Her throat was sore from retching, and to top it all her period had arrived. And then there was the shame of having vomited on the good carpet. What would Susan think when she got up in the morning? "You'd think the old bitch would have managed that much," Bridie said to herself when she saw that it had not been cleaned up. "It'll be impossible to get the stain out now."

The sitting-room stank of cigarette smoke, stale drink and vomit. Bridie opened the windows and sat shivering, a glass of water in front of her. She was half afraid to sip it in case she'd get sick again. After a while she tried to clean the carpet but every time she went near it her stomach began to rise. She spent the rest of the night between the bed and the toilet, her eyes heavy with sleep, her thoughts keeping her awake.

"I'll leave in the morning," she told herself. She corrected that when she realised it was almost morning already. "I'll leave today." She'd stay with her father and mother until she got something else. They could mind Caomhán while she was on the lookout for a job. Maybe even after she started working. There were jobs available in nearly all the factories now, some of them were finding it difficult to recruit enough staff. "Peadar Halloran will give me a job, no bother, in his new factory."

She was too young to spend all her time rearing a child. She'd go to England, learn some skill, make lots of money. Then she wouldn't be dependent on anyone, under a compliment to anyone. "I'll be independent, free," she told herself. She was still mad with Therese. "The least she might have done was clean the carpet when someone was sick. Bloody bitch. Leave it all to the maid, the sweegie, the skivvy. I'd love to dip her pointed nose in it. That'd teach her a thing or two."

She looked in at Caomhán in his cot, and the tears came to her eyes. How could she even think of leaving him? She took him up in her arms and brought him into her own bed. He was all she had, her life. All her plans were suddenly reversed. She didn't mind what she had to do for her baby. She remembered hearing the question asked on some radio programme, "Who would I die for?" She had no problem answering that question. When she'd cried enough, Bridie fell into a deep sleep.

When she woke up about midday Caomhán was no longer beside her. She rushed into the kitchen to find him sitting on Therese's knee, doing a jigsaw puzzle. Bridie grabbed him, took him with her into her room.

"What's wrong with you today?" Therese stood in the open doorway.

"As if you don't know."

"As if I don't know what?"

Bridie changed the subject. "Where's Susan?"

"She left on the ten o'clock bus. She had to play a game of basketball or something. I told her not to waken you, that you didn't have much sleep last night."

Bridie pulled out a suitcase from under the bed.

"What's that for?"

"Guess?"

"What the hell has got into you today, Bridie?"

"Nothing."

"In the name of Jesus."

"I'd appreciate if you didn't take the name of the Lord in vain." Bridie had never complained about bad language before. She felt she needed to latch on to something that might hurt Therese. "If you have neither religion nor morality, it doesn't mean that other people haven't."

"I don't give a fuck about all that," Therese said angrily. "What have I done on you that you're acting the bitch so much this morning, this afternoon, or whatever it is? I thought things were improving between us, that we were becoming better friends. That's why I told you the things I did. I never felt so close to anyone in my life."

"If that's the kind of friend you want, get someone as filthy as yourself."

"I can't help what was done to me when I was small."

"That's not what I'm talking about, and you know it."

"I'm relieved to hear it. So what are you talking about?"

"Is it blind you are, or just plain thick?" Bridie asked.

"Both maybe, but I still don't know what you're getting at."

Bridie spoke slowly, painfully. "I woke up in the middle of the night, last night, in your bed, with your arm around me."

"You'd been very sick, Bridie, and I wanted to make sure you didn't choke on your own vomit."

"You didn't have a stitch of clothes on you. Maybe you don't like men, but I'm not one of them, whatever you call them."

"I get it now," Therese laughed. "You thought I was trying to take advantage of you. If you want to know, it was a lot easier to drag you in there than down here to your own room. And I was genuinely afraid you'd get sick again in your sleep. I could have thrown a blanket over you, and left you lying in your vomit, but I thought you mightn't like Susan to find you like that in the morning."

"Thanks a lot," was the sneering reply.

"You're very welcome." Therese stood, arms akimbo, smiling at her.

"I feel awful today," Bridie said, relenting a little. "My head's killing me. I don't know if I'm coming or going."

"Well, I hope you're not going. Put your bag under the bed, and get a bit of sleep. I'll look after Caomhán until evening."

"Oh, would you? Thanks, Therese."

"Are you sure you wouldn't like me to tuck you in?" Therese joked.

"Don't you dare." She was able to smile about it now.

"You'll recover." Therese quoted Winston Churchill's retort to a woman MP who had accused him of being drunk in the House of Commons. "'You're ugly, madam,' he replied, 'but I'll be sober in the morning.' Sexist and crude," she said to Bridie, "but you know what I mean. You'll feel differently tomorrow."

"PMT is bad enough, without a hangover as well."

"Just as well we don't both have it at the same time, or poor old Caomhán would never stick us."

"At least it'd all be over together." Bridie settled into bed.

"And the two of us murdered at the same time. You'll still have to put up with me later this month."

"Take it out on the crowd in the office."

"I give them enough stick as it is." Therese paused before leaving the bedroom. "Would you like to go for a spin back through Connemara tomorrow?"

"I'd love to, but I'd need to be feeling better than I am today."

"Sleep is the best cure of all; you'll be fine tomorrow." She lifted up Caomhán. "Bye byes to Mammy." He hugged his mother in the bed, and waved bye-bye twenty times before leaving the room.

"Don't forget the warm coat, and his mittens."

"I won't, Mammy," Therese said jokingly. "I mightn't be Mother Hubbard but I'm not a complete idiot with kids."

"You're very good, really," Bridie said, "and thanks for cleaning up the mess."

Therese threw her a mock kiss before closing the door.

It was a cold, bright, windy day with sunny spells between frequent hail showers. Both Caomhán and Therese were well prepared for the November weather, and enjoyed themselves on the empty beach. He had a little plastic bucket and spade, and Therese tried to teach him to make sand castles. He enjoyed knocking them down as quickly as she made them.

They ran races on the strand. Therese pretended that she wasn't able to keep up with him. Caomhán tumbled over himself as often as not, but he enjoyed himself immensely. That was until sand got into his eye. Therese thought she would never manage to console him. The last thing she wanted was to go back to Bridie with a crying child. The tears must have washed out the little grains because he calmed down eventually.

After leaving the beach they strolled up a narrow lane flanked by sycamore trees, an unusual enough sight in the largely treeless landscape west of the

Corrib. A few reluctant leaves still clung to the skeleton branches. Caomhán gripped a couple of fingers of Therese's hand as they walked slowly along. The child's unquestioning trust in the grown-up, she thought. She remembered how she had walked like that with her own father when she wasn't much more than Caomhán's age. She had been full of trust and love.

Her mother was in hospital giving birth to what turned out to be a stillborn baby, her only sister, the first time it happened. She was sitting on his knee listening to a story, enjoying the feeling she got from his fingers as he gently stroked her body, up and down, around and around. He'd kissed her then in a strange kind of way that nearly smothered her, before rising quickly and going to the bathroom.

When he was putting her to bed he had kissed her again in that smothering way. He lay on the bed outside the clothes pushing himself against her, making strange grunting sounds. It was that that frightened her more than anything. She'd asked him not to read any more bedtime stories, she said she knew them all off by heart already. He'd bought a new book for the next night and did the same strange thing again when he finished the story and turned off the light.

Her mother was sad when she came home from the hospital and she stayed in a room of her own most of the time. Her father began to get under the bedclothes and to splash her with some kind of hot liquid when he finished grunting and pushing. He told her not to tell Mammy, that Mammy was ill. She wasn't ready for secrets. This was their secret, and Santa Claus liked little girls who kept secrets. Every single person in the world had a secret, he said, and that was theirs. He liked to lie beside her, he said, because she was his very own little pet, the joy of his life.

Her mother got better and she started to go to bingo on Wednesday nights. This was why Therese still hated Wednesdays. He started sticking that thing into her when she was about six or seven, maybe even as early as five. She still remembered how sore she was on her First Communion day. Her mother had gone out to Confession the previous night, so it was as bad as a Wednesday. "You'll get to like it," he told her once when she told him she didn't like Wednesday nights. "All girls get to like it, except a lot of them never get to do it until they are big, but you're special, my very own pet." He showed her pictures of big people doing the same thing. He said it was the most natural thing in the world, if you loved someone an awful lot.

He'd begun to do it even when her mother was in the house after that so she presumed her mother knew or approved. She thought now that was right. But it seemed to contradict her memory of having to do it quietly, the talk about secrets. She'd a vague memory of him telling her he would take off his belt to her if she made any noise, but in some ways that seemed to be out of character. Still she knew that there was an element of fear there. He never had hit her, never had reason to. He gave her chocolate when she was good, so good she'd always kept their secret.

Therese once heard an expert on the radio quote an eight-year-old child who had been abused. "I liked it down there," the child told the expert, pointing below her waist. "I felt sick in here." She placed a hand on her stomach. Feeling the area of her heart she said, "I felt awful here." And pointing to her head, "I felt guilty about it here." Therese wondered at the ability of an eight-year-old to speak so clearly on the matter. Maybe the doctor was putting words in her mouth; but it did sum up the feelings she had as a young girl. Despite the guilt, despite the mixed emotions, despite everything, she knew she still loved her father. Loved him for who he was, hated him for what he did.

Therese didn't realise she was crying until she noticed Caomhán's big eyes looking up at her. She lifted him up in her arms, and he hugged her tightly. "Nice Teetie," he said. His tune had changed to "Sweetie Teetie," when they got back to the village. She bought him a packet of little chocolate buttons which he smathered all over his face. She sat in a secluded area of one of the pubs drinking a double gin and tonic while he finished off his sweets. She felt better, at least physically. The hair of the dog helped to get rid of the last of her hangover.

They went into the city then and Therese bought two take-aways in the kebab joint at the bottom of Dominick Street, so that there'd be no need to prepare a dinner. Bridie was not too keen on the garlicky taste—her stomach wasn't completely settled, but, though she couldn't eat the food, she appreciated the thought. Bridie went to bed early, intending to turn over a new leaf. She promised herself she'd never allow herself feel as bad as she did that morning. No alcohol ever again, and she would get back to her religious duties, starting with Mass next morning.

Therese had breakfast ready the following morning when Bridie came home from the church. "It's you that's working for me these days," Bridie said, "instead of the other way around."

"Forget about who's working for who, will you, and let's just be friends."

"Whom."

"Whom what?"

"I don't want Caomhán growing up with bad grammar: Who's working for whom."

"For fuck's sake, he can't even say Therese yet."

"You have to start as you want to go on."

"The only thing I want to go on is a spin."

They drove along the coast road through Connemara after lunch, turned north at Casla, out through Camas and Scríb, towards the mountains. The purple and gold of early autumn had turned to deep russet hues around the rosary of lakes that dribble south from Maam. They turned west at Maam Cross. The Twelve Pins looked majestic in the sharp frosty air.

The showers of the previous day had become much less frequent. "Why don't we climb up to Mám Éan?" Therese asked, as they came close to the old Patrician shrine set high among the mountains.

"I don't mind, if you carry Caomhán half the way. There's no way he's going to walk on that rough pathway."

"Some parts of it aren't so bad." Therese pulled on a pair of old wellington boots. "He can walk now and again. It's not far, really."

"For someone that says she has no religion, you seem to know all about it."

"You don't need a formal religion to enjoy such a beautiful place. Come to think of it, Saint Patrick can't have been too bad a bloke when he chose places like this and Croagh Patrick. But then people worshipped here long before Patrick." Therese put Caomhán sitting on her shoulders, a little leg each side of her neck, and her hands went up to hold his.

"Be careful. You'll have no protection if you trip."

"Do you want to carry him first?" That answered that. "Don't worry," Therese said, "I don't want to hurt him any more than you do. Place a little confidence in me some of the time." That said, her foot slipped, and she almost tumbled. "Fuck," she said, a word repeated again and again by Caomhán as they climbed. The women burst their sides laughing at him, which only encouraged more "fucks".

They stood on the height looking south as far as the Burren and the Cliffs of Moher, running like a blue wall beside the sea. The Aran Islands lay like basking sharks across the bay. The water-speckled hills and inlets of south-west Connemara stretched before them like a patchwork quilt. "'How beautiful on the mountains...' I forget the rest of it," Therese said as she looked up at the blue peaks.

"'How beautiful on the mountains are the feet of those who bring good news.'" Bridie remembered her psalm from more recent schooldays, adding, "Saint Patrick must have had a great pair of legs, if that's to be believed."

"That's if you think the news he brought was good news. And speaking of feet, mine are killing me. Would you ever carry this little pudding for a while?" Therese handed over Caomhán and stopped for a moment to massage her thighs, painful from the slow, steep uphill climb.

They walked towards Cliodhna Cussen's big-shouldered limestone statue of Patrick, which stood like a sentry in the little valley. Therese stood with outstretched hands. "Oh, great gods of the mountains," she proclaimed. Caomhán stretched his own arms in imitation. Bridie stood, laughing at both of them.

After a while she asked:

"And who are these gods of yours?"

"The old gods of the Gael, the gods that were worshipped here before Patrick came to rattle the poor snakes."

"Pagan gods?"

"Whatever you want to call them. Personally I think pagan is an insulting, disparaging name. It seems to suggest that they had no truth at all to them."

"Are you saying that they were right?"

"As right as the next crowd, I'd say, according to their own lights. The Christians must have had some respect for their beliefs when they took over all their holy sites."

"They just wanted to do away with the opposition."

"That's one way of looking at it, the way we learned it, I suppose. I think they had enough sense to recognise a holy place when they saw it, to realise that it was essentially the same god people worshipped before and after Patrick."

"I don't know," Bridie shrugged, "if there's any god at all."

"I seem to remember you going to Mass this morning."

"That's what disgusted me, an old man going on about private intimate things that he knows nothing about, condemning, giving out."

"Maybe he's learned a lot from life."

"You've got very tolerant all of a sudden." Bridie was sarcastic. "We should come here oftener."

"Old Jack Jordan isn't the worst."

"It would do him good to go up on a woman and learn what it's all about before he starts giving out about rubber johnnies. He had some funny name for them, prophylactics, I think. Some of the ould ones must have thought it was a new kind of a prophet. Though he did manage to mention condoms a few times. I'd like to see him and his likes up to their ears in dirty nappies."

"Isn't he a happy man when you think of it, that has nothing but sex to worry him from morning till night."

"You're slagging him off yourself now." Bridie looked back at her, laughing. "You can be a right bitch when you want to."

Therese had been leading Caomhán by the hand for some time. She was trying to get him to walk as far as possible on their way back down the mountain, to give him some exercise as well as to give themselves a rest. She lifted him up and carried him a hundred yards or so but she was getting tired. "Will you take this little fellow for a while, Bridie? It'll be dark in an hour, and I'd hate to be stuck on the mountain with no one for company but Saint Patrick."

"Not to speak of your own gods," Bridie teased her as she took Caomhán, letting him sit against her waist, one leg on each side of her hip.

"I'm afraid they've gone to sleep too, like the rest of the gods."

The orange sun was ready to drop into the Atlantic when they got back to the car. Therese drove as far as Ballinahinch Castle, where they drank hot punch before the great log fire in the downstairs bar. They ate smoked salmon sandwiches in fresh brown bread, and Caomhán gobbled the salmon as if there was no tomorrow.

"There's nothing like the mountain air to give a man an appetite." Bridie broke yet another sandwich into little pieces. He grabbed with both hands, literally stuffing his face with food.

"Fingers were made before forks." Therese laughed at him.

Two old men began to chat with them in Irish when they heard the women speak that language between themselves. The men had been at a funeral of an old friend that day in Recess and they sat remembering the man that was gone.

"A pity he's not here now. That's the man that would keep Irish with you," one of them said with a mixture of pride and sadness.

"You're well able to spout it out yourself," was Therese's reply.

"We knew it once, the old people spoke nothing else when we were growing up, but sure it died out around here a long time ago."

"You'd never know," Bridie said optimistically, "it might make a comeback one of these days, like what's happening in the all-Irish schools in Dublin and Derry and all around the country."

"Sure the children isn't in it to teach," the older-looking of the men said.

"A pity they never did anything with the school beyond." Therese touched on a raw nerve when she mentioned a controversy that hit the national headlines ten years before, a dispute about teaching through Irish which led to the boycotting of the Principal Teacher, and eventually to the closing of the school.

"That's all like water under the bridge outside now." The men hurriedly finished their pints and left.

"They must think we're reporters or something," Therese laughed. "Isn't history a strange thing too.

The people around here'll never live down pulling the carriage out of the bog for an English King or Lord Lieutenant or something. I can't remember exactly who it was now. They're branded forever as some kind of shoneens because they did someone a good turn when his horses got stuck in the bog."

"They should have left him in it," was Bridie's curt reply.

"So much for tolerance."

"They weren't too tolerant to the teacher on her own beyond in the schoolroom."

"We'd better get out of here," Therese was looking around the empty bar, "before you start a riot or something."

"I suppose you can't paint everyone anywhere with the same brush," Bridie conceded resignedly.

"I enjoyed that." Therese finished her drink, holding the glass above her head until the last drop was drained.

"That was a lovely day." Bridie sat back, relaxed, in what reminded her of the teacher's chair at the national school. "I thought yesterday morning that I'd never feel good again. They're right about drink. It's a fierce depressive."

"Said she, swallowing her punch," Therese laughed.

"I know I did swear that I'd never touch the stuff again... Ah, but this is lovely all the same. There's no harm in one or two. I certainly never want to feel the way I felt yesterday ever again."

"That's life, up today and down tomorrow, or vice versa." Therese stood up. "Well, all good things must come to an end. We have a long road ahead of us."

No sooner was he in the car than Caomhán was asleep lying flat out on the back seat. The two women didn't speak much. Therese concentrated on the road. Bridie was lost in her own thoughts. They were almost in Oughterard on the straight road to Galway when Bridie said thoughtfully, "Isn't it strange how when you're feeling down, you think you'll never snap out of it?"

"I suppose many a one commits suicide at a time like that," Therese said. "Another day and they would feel differently."

"You don't be like that?"

"Who doesn't?"

"Really?"

"Not much in recent times, except when the PMT is like TNT ready to explode inside me, but I thought of it a lot when I was young."

"Because of your father?"

"A couple of times when we were at the seaside, back there in Dog's Bay a few miles from where we had the drink. I thought of just letting myself sink, forget about everything, put an end to it all."

"But you didn't," Bridie felt her own question was stupid, "obviously."

"I believed in hell-fire that time. It could hardly have been much worse than the hell I was living through."

Bridie didn't reply. She didn't know what to say.

They managed to carry Caomhán into the house without wakening him, and put him straight to bed. "I'll change him later before I go down myself," Bridie said. "You know I felt today as if the three of us were our own little family."

"Does that make me the Daddy?" Therese joked.

"I've heard it said that you have more balls than anyone on the Board; maybe that's what they meant."

"Reminds me of a joke."

"Not a dirty one, I hope," Bridie smiled.

"What other kind is there? And after what you've just said."

"Tell me."

"I was out in Spain last year on a Gaeltacht Board junket." Therese had a twinkle in her eye as she told her story. "We had a meal in a fancy restaurant, and decided to try the cojones from the menu."

"And what are cojones when they're at home?"

"Have patience, my dear," Therese gave a theatrical flourish with her right hand, "all will be revealed in due course. Anyway, they tasted lovely, a little bit like prawns done in garlic butter."

"They must have made you stink."

"We enjoyed the meal so much that we went back to the same place the following night, and ordered cojones again. They were disgusting, small little yokeens like snails floating in a drop of olive oil."

"Did you complain?" Bridie knew that Therese wouldn't have anything second-rate pawned off on her.

"Of course we did, and do you know all the satisfaction we got?"

"I don't know, but I'm sure you're going to tell me."

"'The toreador, he does not always win,' the waiter told us."

Bridie thought for a moment. "Bollocks," she said.

"Precisely," said Therese, smiling and bowing her head.

"Cojones or no," Bridie said, "you've done a lot for the area since you came back from England."

"I happened to get the job at the right time," was the modest reply.

"You were earning a lot more over there?"

"What good is money if a person isn't satisfied?"

"I wouldn't turn down money like that."

"That's what you think now," Therese told her. "In years to come you'll look at these years as the best time of your life, when you were struggling, but succeeding to rear Caomhán."

"That sounds like saying that your schooldays are the happiest days of your life. My happiest schoolday was the day I finished," Bridie said, emphatically.

"Well, today was a very happy day for me." Therese gave Bridie a peck on the cheek as she passed her, on her way to bed. "Our own little family out for a spin."

"Jesus, Mary and Joseph," Bridie said jokingly, sarcastically.

❧

On Sunday John took the London Underground to Piccadilly. He spent a while walking the streets, looking in the shop windows, just being part of the crowd that thronged the pavements. In some ways it reminded him of the wonder he used to feel as a small boy when his mother would take him with her shopping in Galway city. Everything seemed new and exciting after the drabness of prison. "I must look like an eejit," he said to himself when he found he was standing back to look up at the tall buildings.

People of every kind and colour walked the streets, sober traditional suits mixing with the flamboyant colours of the East. Indians, Pakistanis, Greeks, Turks, you name it, he thought. "Well, there's at least one Paddy among them." He wondered why so many people seemed to be in such a hurry on a Sunday morning. Maybe it's just to keep warm, he thought, as he felt the icy blast of the wind from side streets. It seemed strange to see people rushing around when he was just trying to pass the time.

A one-legged middle-aged man sat on the cold concrete footpath painting a picture in coloured chalk. John walked across the picture, turning his heel on the face the man had drawn. John knew in his heart and soul that this was an ugly and cowardly thing to do. He didn't know why he did it, and hated the vicious streak in him that led him to hurt the harmless man. He just felt like doing it at the time. John didn't know what language the man spoke angrily at him but he'd no doubt he was being roundly cursed.

For a moment he thought of turning back, apologising, but thought better of it. After the IRA bombing on the Underground two weeks previously, people with Irish accents were anything but popular. A man could be assaulted for opening his mouth. "Those bad bastards give every decent Irishman a bad name," he thought as he hurried across to the other side of the square.

John went into a pizza "palace" that seemed to be as big as a football pitch, but despite its size it was difficult to find an empty table. He felt lonely among all these people. He couldn't wait for Christmas, to be back among his own, to what he thought was natural. He was like a fish out of water here. He had more than enough of the big city life. He blamed it for all his problems. He thought of Bridie and their child. "Wait until she hears that I haven't had a drink in two years," he said to himself.

The Cockneys in prison had talked of the great skip of drink he'd have the day he got out. Although he'd let them think that he'd drink London dry, he hadn't touched a drop. He'd felt he was being faithful to Bridie, to the future. Going back on the drink would have been like going to a prostitute that night. Despite the temptations, he'd given in to neither. That showed a bit of backbone, the kind of discipline he intended to practise from now on.

"Daddy," he said to himself aloud, as he thought of the little fellow, the little fellow that must be a big fellow now. He'd got into the habit of speaking out loud to himself in the cell. People at nearby tables looked at him in surprise. "I'm a Daddy," he told them to cover his embarrassment. "My wife has just given birth to a baby boy." His accent didn't matter then. It was as if he had the baby in his arms. For a moment it looked as if he was going to get a round of applause.

People warmed to him, congratulated him. It was as if he'd single-handedly broken the ice in the pizza palace. *When a child is born* was being played on the public address. No wonder the Christmas story was so attractive, a baby got everyone gurgling. He hurried out in case he'd run out of white lies, contradict himself about his new-born two-year-old babe.

Back on the streets John imagined himself teaching the young fellow to play football like a real Daddy. He thought of his son playing for Galway. "I might play for them yet myself, if the selectors don't find out about the prison sentence." Maybe the GAA would have a hang-up about respectability, but then they couldn't ignore him if he got back to playing the way he used to.

His home county needed some football success. The legend of the magic three-in-a-row team of the sixties had worn thin with the years; only the hurlers had brought glory to the county for more than three decades now. "Our day will come again, and guess who'll be the hero?"

He was playing now for Galway in Croke Park before seventy thousand people, Galway against Kerry, two of football's aristocrats back at the top again after the lean years. A high ball floated in towards the square. Even though the full-back had a grip on his jersey, John positioned himself perfectly under the dropping ball. Instead of rising high as he usually did, he took the ball on his chest. A quick shuffle of his feet had his marker floundering, clawing and pawing at him.

The referee played advantage, he outpaced the full-back, chipped the goalkeeper, who landed on his backside as he anticipated a low hard shot. John ran out towards centrefield, a clenched fist in the air, to roars of adulation from a success-starved maroon and white flag-waving support. The chant of "Gal-way, Gal-way" changed to "John, John, John." Prison, drinking, all was forgiven at that moment.

He'd brought daydreams to perfection in prison. You could forget about the blue-grey walls and be anywhere you wanted to be. He was able to bring Croke Park to Piccadilly as he walked the streets. How many prison days had he spent in Connemara? At school he'd heard that James Joyce had carried Dublin with him to the continent. John had done the same with the heathery hills and broad sweep of Atlantic that was home. It had kept him sane in the dark days.

But what was he to do for the rest of the day? He had decided not to go back to the little bedsitter until after nightfall. The lonely streets were better than that any day. He couldn't even chance a soft drink in a public bar. "The temptation to go on the piss would be too great," he thought. A squally shower of sleet was starting. When he was looking around for a place to shelter he noticed the gaudy entrance to a cinema. What about seeing a film? It would pass a while of the day.

If the picture was no good he could have a sleep in a warm, comfortable place, he thought. He paid a couple of pounds to the bored-looking but pretty girl at the entrance. He had his choice of seats. There were only a handful of customers scattered around the cinema. "Sure it's still only dinnertime," he told himself, "or lunch time as they call it over here."

John got a shock when he sat down and looked up at the screen. A man and a woman, both stark naked, were screwing away for all they were worth on a kitchen table, oblivious to the noise of breaking delph, as plates, saucers and cups were pushed or kicked to the floor by their coupling. They had it bad, he thought enviously.

In spite of himself he felt guilty about watching a dirty movie. He thought he should walk out, but couldn't take his eyes off the screen. What really amazed him was the fact that the place was almost empty despite the exciting carry-on on the screen. The stuff that couple got up to on and off the table had to be seen to be believed.

Then it was a threesome, four, five in all sorts of contortions and positions, arse over head and head over arse. They hadn't a bit of shame in them, John thought, as he settled down to see what they'd get up to next. Two women tied a man who had been following them to a tree, took down his pants, and took turns to hammer a job on him. Then they tied a bunch of flowers to his willy and left him like that. "I wouldn't mind being captured by the pair of them," John thought.

A man couldn't watch the likes of that for long without getting horny. He was bursting out of his pants. There was no one near him so he opened his fly and pumped himself until he sprayed out against the back of the seat in front of him. What choice had he? You couldn't go out on the streets of London with a big wet patch on your trousers. After a little while he slipped across to the next row, in case the lights would come on to find the evidence of his frustration reflecting like snow from the back of the seat.

He'd never thought that he'd tire of looking at the likes of that, but when he awoke from a snooze it was nearly five o'clock. The same carry-on took place on the screen, no real story to it. He didn't even know whether the film had restarted or if he was watching the same thing all over again. It looked familiar. He laughed to himself when he realised that he hadn't been looking at the faces anyway. "When you've seen one bare arse," he thought, "you've seen them all."

It was cold on the streets, and he felt hungry. John turned in the door of the next chipper he saw. "Double hamburger and chips." Prices had really soared in the couple of years he'd been inside. He had to go rooting for more change in his pockets. The hot crispy chips were like manna from heaven, but the bunburgers were bland and almost tasteless. "Home-cooking, here I come," he thought, as he looked forward to his mother serving up a big basketful of steaming potatoes on the table in the old-fashioned way.

It had been a long day. He couldn't wait to be back next morning at the training job the probation officer had got for him. The words of an old song kept running through his mind, "Something about a Sunday makes a body feel alone." He compared his day to a Sunday back home, morning Mass, a match, the dance, tending to farm animals in between. A busy, fulfilling day.

"Oh, Jesus," he thought, "I never thought of going to Mass." That was one thing he had promised the prison chaplain. "Keep up the prayers," the man had never tired of saying, "and you won't put a foot wrong outside." John had liked him even though the other fellows thought he was off the wall, too much of a wimp to make any impression on street-wise young criminals. But he'd seemed to care. "It's not too late yet," John thought, "there are bound to be evening Masses in a big city."

Back on the street he stopped a well-dressed man to ask where he might find a Catholic church. For a second he thought the man was getting some kind of apoplexy as his face screwed up in hate. "Fuck off, you dirty Paddy," the man spat out the words as he angrily raised his umbrella. "Murdering bastards!" John walked quickly away, desperately trying not to attract attention. People were already stopping to see what all the commotion was about.

John was still shaking with the shock of the man's reaction to his Irishness when he went into the first church he saw. It was warm and comfortable, and as he began to relax again he realised that it was not evening Mass but Evensong. "Fuck this for a crack," he said to himself, but then decided to stay. The hymns had a Christmassy feel to them, real Christmas compared to the commercial stuff pumped out on the radio and from every record shop and café you passed by.

Maybe the prison chaplain was right. There was very little difference between Catholic and Protestant. It was small enough things that divided them. "You couldn't tell that to the crowd in Northern Ireland," he thought. But he remembered the chaplain's words, "We all believe in the same God, in Jesus as saviour, in the Holy Spirit." In the "whole lot" as John himself would have put it. He had thought a lot of that chaplain, he spoke sense, not like a lot of the clergy back home. There was a sense of peace there in this Protestant chapel far from home.

"Amn't I the right buck too," he laughed to himself as he thought back on his day, "going from a dirty picture to a Protestant church." What would his mother make of it all? She'd think he was damned for all eternity and she'd grind out a good few Rosaries to make up for all that. Still it was better than being out drinking, or looking for the ride. After all he was a married man.

All he wanted from now on was Bridie. He'd never look at another woman again. He'd have gone to Confession on the spot, got absolution for his wank in the cinema, except that the Protestants didn't go in for it. "The two religions were not as alike as your man the chaplain made out," he thought. "Confession was a great job too, the slate wiped clean in a couple of minutes."

He thought of going back to Cricklewood, looking up some of his own mates. But they'd have no time for a man who wasn't drinking. "No wimps need apply," was the first rule of their club. He thought of them now with a certain contempt, slaving all week in muck and dirt, drawing a "sub" every evening for drink, having most of their wages spent before the end of the week. A weekend of pubs and bookies, lots of talk about sex but never doing anything about it. Always planning to go back home, for Christmas, for the summer, never being able to afford to, never able to break their own vicious circles.

He'd worked with men who had come over in the fifties and sixties who were still "lads". They'd never married, never done anything, except work, sleep, drink. One of these days they were going to do something. It was not just "back yonder," as Ireland was known, that was full of middle-aged bachelors. A lot of men who had emigrated looked the very same in any pub you went into in Kilburn, Camden or Kentish Town on a weekend: Sunday suits, cloth caps, talk of Gaelic football, hurling, women, "just like back yonder." John didn't plan to end up like one of them.

"Six weeks to Christmas. How will I ever stick it?" As he headed back to the Underground he consoled himself with the thought that time passed quickly in the training centre during the week. It was the weekends that were the killers. He thought of getting a part-time job in a bar or café. It would pass the time and bring in a few pounds extra.

"Like to have a good time, love?" She was tall, blonde, thin, leggy in a red leather miniskirt, boots coming above her knees. "She must be frozen with the cold," he thought, as he looked at her skimpy clothes. "Well, I won't be warming her." He smiled. "No, thanks, ma'am, I'm married."

"When did that make any difference?"

"It makes a difference to me, luv." He tried to put on an English accent as he remembered the rage of the man outside the café. The wank in the cinema seemed like a blessing in disguise to him now. If he hadn't had that relief he'd have been tempted to take up the offer of "a good time". It would be a bad time to pick up some kind of a pox when he had high hopes of getting back with his own wife.

At the station he bought a couple of Sunday tabloid papers and read bits and pieces of them as the tube train lurched quickly along. Irish people were still in the bad books. There was talk of identity cards, passports. An old couple in Fulham who'd been in England since before the war had their windows smashed. An Irish international soccer player had been booed at the Arsenal-Tottenham match in Highbury. That explosion had left an ugly taste. The sooner he was back home, the better.

When it came to sport though, the tabloid papers were really interesting. Anything the professional footballer did on or off the field came under scrutiny. It made them heroes really, royalty nearly. Both seemed to have the same fascination for the British public. John felt that it was a pity Gaelic footballers weren't treated like that back home. They got very little return for all the work they put in.

As he lay on his bed in the narrow attic room watching the stars winking through the skylight, John felt happy. For some reason the sight of the stars reminded him of his childhood, when life was magic. Everything from a hen to a cowshit was exotic, worth exploring. Anything and everything was possible. He wondered would it be the same for his own little fellow?

Many things in his life had turned sour on him in recent years, but a lot of his dreams had come true too. He was always the best at sport, a natural athlete, the schoolmaster had said. Maybe things had come too easily to him in that field; he'd never had to struggle like a lot of the other fellows had. He'd known fellows who would have given an arm and a leg to represent the school, the club, the county, but they just didn't have the ability. He'd taken things like that for granted until he left school, but he'd never gone beyond that. It had never mattered enough to him.

He sometimes wondered had he things too easy in his younger days. People in the country always said the youngest of the family was the pet. He'd never felt like the pet but maybe he was. He never had to work as hard as his older brothers or sisters at hay or on the bog, because they were always there. They were bigger, the girls worked as hard as the boys, especially in the years after his father's early death. Because he was needed by the football club, John had often taken his football gear and gone off to training when the others were going to the meadow.

He saw himself now as a little boy on the road to school, standing near a rusted gate listening to a bird that seemed to be calling his name: "Seáinín, Seáinín." That's what he was called as a boy, to distinguish him from his father, who was also Seán. His father's death and the fact that he was big for his age made the "ín" a contradiction. Then the schoolmistress took to calling him "John," because there was another Seán in the class, and the name had stuck.

He found out later that the bird that seemed to call his name was the curlew, a bird he felt some kind of affinity with as it swooped over the bog calling for rain. There was another bird with a strange cry which he associated with the low boggy field they called the turlough, a bird that sounded like a kid goat. He wasn't the only one to think so. The bird was called *mionnári aerach* in Irish, the flying kid.

Memories like that reminded him of happy times at home. Some day his little boy would recognise those birds and know them by name too. His son would watch the the heron or *cradhain fhada* flap lazily across the bog as he helped his father cut the turf. He'd listen to the lark trilling high notes in the blue skies of Connemara, know the cuckoo, the swallow, the robin and the wren. Maybe a magic bird would call his name too. Whatever that was. Some day soon he would know.

John hadn't felt so content and happy in himself for a long time as he did that night. Despite the loneliness and boredom of the day he hadn't yielded to the temptation of the booze. That was the main thing. The cause of all his problems was there for the taking all around him, but he had been strong. He had resisted. Bridie would be proud of him. "One day at a time," he told himself, "and today is done. With God's help I'll get them back, my wife and child. We'll be the happiest family in all the west of Ireland yet." With that positive thought he slept.

❧

Therese tore into the offices of the Gaeltacht Board like a hurricane on Monday morning. She blew greetings left and right, apparently bright and good-humoured, noticing at the same time who was in and who was not. God help the employee who hadn't a good excuse for absence from work on a Monday morning, especially if she'd seen them out drinking or socialising over the weekend.

She wouldn't say anything when they came in. But she'd give them extra work in the evening, flexitime they had to do or they would know it in their pay-packets. It didn't matter whether it was office work, building work or factory work. The same rules applied to everyone in the organisation, herself included. Physical presence was not enough, when you were at work you were expected to work.

Because she'd been away touring the Gaeltacht the previous Friday, there was a lot of correspondence. With a cup of coffee in her hand she paced the office, dictating replies. By the time she'd signed the letters it was time for the eleven o'clock coffee break.

In the canteen Therese was one of the girls, discussing the weekend's happenings, who was going with whom, were such and such an "item", what was this dance or that session like. At twenty past eleven she was first out of the canteen. The others followed her quickly back to their desks.

Sometimes she felt the staff must think she was a right bitch. But she knew it was important to scotch for ever the notion that Irish workers were lazy, slow or both. Irish people had proved all over the world that they were as good as if not better than the next in business matters if the incentives and the rewards were right. Despite that there seemed to be a perception in European capitals that the Irish were too laid-back to be effective. Thatch wanted to prove that her staff worked, and that they worked hard.

She reached for the file marked "Teilifís na Gaeltachta". A proper television service for the Gaeltacht and Irish-speakers generally was her first priority. Young people would show little interest in a language that wasn't part of their lives, part of the television culture. The local population was increasing and the pressure on the old language was stronger than ever.

The couple of hours a day devoted mainly to children's programming introduced some years earlier as Teilifís na Gaeilge needed to be expanded now as those children became young adults. That particular service had been aimed primarily at urban middle-class youngsters going to all-Irish schools. It seemed to have no significant impact on the youth of the traditional Irish-speaking areas.

While fluent in both Irish and English, the young people seldom spoke anything but English among themselves in any school-yard in the Gaeltacht. The strange thing was that many went back to Irish when they settled down and married. Most tried to rear their children through Irish, but their children voted with their tongues. Almost everything of interest in the television world was in English. A proper full-scale Irish language service might not save the language in the Gaeltacht, but there was no hope without it.

Therese realised that political pressure was building up to prevent the introduction of the type of independent service she had in mind. Politicians were quick to realise that power was connected with media control, subtle or strong. Nothing threatened the old conservative ways more than a television service outside state control. The Government would far prefer to pay for a state service than have an independent self-financing one.

Therese was well aware of the effort made the previous year to have her hounded out of her job. They'd planted stories in tabloid papers. They said she'd had a relationship with an IRA man on the wanted list in London. It was suggested that this was the real reason why she'd given up a good job to come back to a rural backwater. The Irish language connection was used as further proof of her perverted patriotism. She'd given the money she won in the libel action to the Galway Rape Crisis Centre.

Something like that seemed to be starting again. She'd been shown a tabloid heading from one of yesterday's newspapers, *Blonde wants own TV station*. Proceedings of the previous week's Gaeltacht Board were reported verbatim, a clear indication that a Board member had broken the confidentiality rule. "Does the noble language of the Gael allow any and every terrorist express themselves on the airwaves?" the editorial asked.

"When did that bloody rag ever show interest in the noble language of the Gael?" she asked herself. "When had they ever published a line in that language? Lousy hypocrites." It wasn't the paper that angered her so much as the Board member who spilled the beans. She had hoped to have been able to go to the Minister with a *fait accompli*, a TV service, self-financing and ready to run.

There would be little he could do to stop it then, given the high-quality, high-tech jobs it would create in the locality, with feeder stations in the other Gaeltacht areas. She told herself to be careful, not to give the Minister, the Board members or the newspapers any stick to beat her with.

Shaking off her anger, Therese rang Bridie, to ask how she was, to ask about Caomhán. This was something she'd never thought of doing previously. It wasn't that she needed to do it. She'd seen them a couple of hours ago but she felt close to them. It was nice to let people know you were thinking of them. Her family—she thought of them like that—were more important to her than her work, than political pressure. Thinking of them put all the other things in perspective. It gave her a life outside her job. Bridie was delighted to get her call.

"This is the second nice thing to happen me since morning," she said. She told Therese that Peadar Halloran had phoned some time earlier, and invited her to the GAA social on the following Friday night.

"I didn't realise that the two of you were that great. I'll soon need eyes in the back of my head to keep up with the goings on of the two of you." Bridie was too excited to notice the coolness that had crept into Therese's voice.

"We're not great at all, but it's nice to be asked out all the same. I have nothing to wear or anything."

"You *are* going out with him then?"

"I didn't give him a straight answer until I know about a baby-sitter. Susan is in the quiz final in the youth club so she can't do it." Bridie hoped Therese would offer to care for Caomhán on the night but she didn't want to ask her straight out if she'd do it. The offer was not forthcoming. Therese made an excuse about having to get back to work now. The phone was hung up.

Bridie didn't know what to think of the invitation. She reminded herself that she was a married woman. She knew she wouldn't go back to John again. "Anyway, Peadar is more like a brother than anything else," she told herself, though what he'd said about fancying her worried her slightly. "But what's wrong with that either?" she asked her image in the mirror. "A cat can look at a queen. You can look at the menu without partaking."

The funny thing was that she thought of Peadar more as if he was one of the girls than as a fellow. "If he heard me," she said aloud to Caomhán, who sat on his potty giving little grunts, though he showed little interest until then in toilet training. But it was true for her. The lads from her class at school were different from the others, friends rather than fellows you'd fancy.

Therese stood at her office window, looking out across the bay. The blue-grey bulk of Clare's Burren seemed close, and the Aran Islands to the west of it stood out a clear dark blue from the sea. A sign of rain, the old people would say, although the sky was still clear and the sea calm. "Why," she asked herself, "does it disturb me that Bridie would want to go out with Peadar Halloran, or anyone else?" Why should she be jealous of anything Bridie did? But they had been getting so close, and she was afraid that this could come between them.

"Silly bitch," she chided herself for thinking such thoughts as she looked out at the Aran Islands stretched across the mouth of the big bay. Therese thought of the girls from the islands who had shared her years in Tourmakeady College while it was still a boarding school. It had seemed so strange that fellow-students should have to travel by boat, or in later times by plane as well as by bus, while the rest of them were driven there by their parents. The difficulties of island life seemed to give those girls an extra resilience and grace, prepared them for any hardship.

Then she looked directly across Galway Bay at the great rounded shoulder of Black Head at the outer

edge of the slate-blue Burren. A magical place, she said
to herself, remembering the effect Mullach Mór had
on her the first time she saw that distinctive mountain
that had caused controversy, curses and the loss of
parliamentary seats in the early years of the nineties.

She thought of what she had said the previous day
at Mám Éan about the gods of the Gael. They were her
gods, Gael and Gaeltacht, but the first of all her gods
was her work, and here she was daydreaming. "Don't
be daft," she told herself, "get back to work." It was
unusual for her to find her thoughts wandering in the
middle of a working day. She returned quickly to her
desk.

Bridie failed to find a baby-sitter on the night of the
GAA social. She'd thought at first that she might be
able to leave her child with her father and mother for
the night. Of all nights in the year they were going to
the pensioners' party. They didn't get out much so
Bridie didn't even ask them. They'd probably have
stayed at home specially to look after their grandson.

Although she had mentioned her difficulties many
times, Therese never offered to mind Caomhán. To
compound Bridie's anger, she hadn't gone out at all
herself, just sprawled on the couch watching the *Late
Late Show*. "It wouldn't have cost her anything to have
minded him," she thought gloomily, as she went to
bed early and angry.

"Why don't we take a spin down to Coole Park?"
Therese asked airily on the following morning.

"I don't feel like it. I have a headache." She didn't
allow Caomhán to go either, saying that the weather

was very broken, that she was afraid he would get a cold. They'd hardly spoken a word all day.

Peadar Halloran called to ask Bridie out any night of the week. She tried every excuse in the book to put him off. "Name your night," he said; "you can't be that tied down. There must be a baby-sitter you can get some time. Everyone is entitled to a bit of a night out now and again." She didn't promise anything.

"You know my number," he said.

"I'll give you a ring some time," she said vaguely.

"Sometime is nevertime," he said crossly before he hung up.

"Who was it?" Therese asked when Bridie came in to the sitting-room.

"Isn't it you that's curious."

"Interested might be more like it, especially when I heard you trying to put someone off. It sounded like I have you tied down here."

"I didn't think anyone would be listening," Bridie said, pointedly.

"I couldn't help overhearing. Who was it anyway?"

"A friend." She didn't know why she was too embarrassed to say Peadar's name.

"Is that fellow still following you around like a little poodle?"

"I don't know who you're talking about."

"That Halloran fellow."

"I don't think it's nice to compare anyone to a dog."

"It's impossible to talk to you today."

"Well, even if the poodle is following me, it doesn't own me, or me him." Bridie's mood softened when she remembered a joke commonly told in her area about one of the old characters. One day the sergeant asked him had he a licence for his dog. "Sure that dog isn't mine at all," the old man had replied. "He must be," said the sergeant, "isn't he following you?" The old man had his answer, "You're following me too, and you're not mine." The ice was broken by the laughter and they were friends again.

They drove to Coole Park the following day, to Cong the following Sunday, the Saturday after that to Westport, stopping for coffee on the way back in the beautiful pub at Maam Bridge. Patrick Pearse had stayed there once while on a bicycle tour with a girlfriend, a point stressed in one biography to prove that he wasn't homosexual. Christmas was fast approaching and they went shopping in Galway on the eighth of December. This was a Catholic Church holiday and the Gaeltacht Board workers had a free day.

"I thought it'd be against your principles to take a church holiday off," Bridie teased.

"I never said the Church wasn't good for something."

As children had that day off school, the city was crowded with people doing their Christmas shopping. There were decorations everywhere, the lights had just been switched on. Caomhán loved the excitement and the colour. Everywhere he looked he saw something that attracted him. He spent most of his time pointing, and saying, *"Breathnaigh!"*

Therese looked after him for a while, carrying him around the craft fair as Bridie slipped away to buy him his present from Santa. He was still a bit too young to understand what all the excitement was about, but children probably didn't think like that. Excitement was excitement. Magic was magic. There were probably no ifs or buts or whys in his mind at that stage. Bridie wondered if she herself and Therese were enjoying the season even more than the child they said they were doing it all for.

They brought Caomhán into Santa's cave in the biggest of the shopping centres. He refused point blank to go up on the old man's knee, only doing so when Bridie sat on the opposite knee. They managed a couple of pictures as he tried to squirm away from this strange man with the big white beard. They spent more and more time together. Therese used the excuse of not wanting to disturb people's Christmas to reduce her night-time meetings to a trickle.

"Soon we won't have anywhere else to go." They were in Roundstone the following Sunday, walking the great beach of Dog's Bay, wrapped warmly in their winter woollies.

"We'll just start all over again," Therese answered. "Places change from season to season, from week to week, nearly." She looked at her watch. "The day's far too short at this time of the year, though. We'd better get a few miles out of it before it gets dark."

They took the coast road this time, winding around bays and across bogs, stopping at the fall of night at Tigh Chite in Derrynea. They were within striking distance of home, so they sat by the open fire in the lounge, sipping a couple of hot whiskeys. Therese made sure not to drink any more than the limit allowed drivers. "Isn't it a great life too," Bridie smiled, looking down on Caomhán sleeping on her lap. They were going to have a lovely Christmas. All was right with her world.

A letter came the next day containing a bank draft for £500. The accompanying note was short. "Dear

Bridie, Buy something nice for the young fellow for Christmas. Love, John." For a moment she thought she might faint. He was out. She felt a cold sweat on her back. "I'll have to tell Therese," was her first thought.

The girl in the Gaeltacht Board office said that the Chief Executive was not available. Bridie left a message to tell her to ring back as soon as she got in. Therese came on the phone within seconds. "What's wrong?"

"I got a letter from John."

"John who?"

"My husband. My ex."

"Fuck John," Therese said angrily. "You mean to tell me you rang just to tell me you got a letter from your husband. I'm busy here, Bridie. I have a lot on my plate. There's a big shot down from the Minister's office. I thought the house was on fire, or that the child had fallen or something."

"But you don't understand..." Bridie didn't have time to finish her sentence.

"It's you that doesn't understand, Bridie. I have a job to do. See you this evening."

"Fuck you and your job," Bridie said to the dead phone, throwing the receiver from her. Soon afterwards she saw Caomhán throwing down one of his toys, saying, "Fuck you," in imitation of his mother.

She looked again at John's envelope. She examined the postmark. At least he was still in London. Maybe he'd stay there. There was no address on the note. She wouldn't be able to send the money back to him. She thought of throwing it in the fire but it wasn't an easy thing to do when you were struggling to exist. She'd wait until Therese came home before she decided to do anything. At this stage she felt embarrassed that she'd phoned the office at all. She hoped that Therese wouldn't be too vexed with her.

Bridie worked hard all evening to have the place clean, warm and cosy when Therese returned. She prepared her favourite meal, Chicken Kiev and chips. There wasn't much imagination to it, Bridie thought, having bought the meat already garlicked and bread-crumbed in the butcher's, but a person liked what they liked. "She'll eat the head off me for sure when she comes in, and who could blame her?"

It wasn't like that. Therese was very sorry indeed. She said she was under a bit of pressure at the time. Some of the newspapers had been on to the Minister's office, following up the tabloid story of a few weeks back. He'd sent his top man down to investigate but things seemed to have gone well. Someone somewhere was keeping the pot boiling, keeping the pressure on as the day approached when plans for the new service would be put to the Board.

"Was your man mad when I rang?"

"Don't worry," Therese laughed, "I turned it to my own advantage, told him it was part of a most important deal that I was playing hard to get in on."

"I forget half the time that the job can put you under pressure," Bridie said. "It's just that you seem so confident and sure of yourself. I never thought for a minute that anything like that would upset you."

"Well, you were more upset than I was." Therese dismissed the matter. "What did your man say in the letter anyway?"

She laughed at the idea that Bridie might return the money or burn the cheque. "It's the least he might do for his son. What has he given up until now? Nothing."

"I suppose he couldn't do much from prison."
Bridie was surprised to find herself defending John.

"It shows he cares a bit about him anyway."

"If he's not just trying to manipulate me. Doesn't
it put me under a compliment, under an obligation to
him?"

"It wasn't you he sent it for, but for Caomhán.
Shouldn't every man support his child, whether he's
single, married or divorced."

"But what am I to do if he comes back?"

"We'll come to that one when it happens, if it
happens. You're not alone in this, Bridie. Anyway I
think the shame of being in jail for battering you
won't let him show his face around here again."

"I don't think shame is a thing John understands."

"You don't mean to tell me you love him still?"
Therese's question came as a bit of a shock to Bridie.

"Love? Not alone do I not love him, I'm afraid of
him. I suppose the reason I got such a shock today was
because I've hardly even thought of him for a long
time. Things were going fine with us. I was never
happier, preparing for Christmas and everything. And
now this."

"Don't worry about what might never happen."

"Next thing he'll be coming looking for his 'rights'
as he calls them."

"He can't force you to do anything."

"You don't know John."

"One thing sure," Therese said determinedly, "if he
does come back, he won't be allowed come around
here without an invitation from you. Not unless he
wants to end up in prison again. There is a law in the
land."

"The law can do nothing until damage is done," Bridie answered, "as I well know."

"There is this law here too." Therese raised the poker.

"That would be useless with John. He's as strong as a bull."

"There's many a way to stop the likes of him." Therese was trying to console Bridie. "Scald the balls off him with a kettle of boiling water."

"You don't understand, Therese. You just freeze in front of someone like him. You're afraid to defend yourself in case he does something worse. He could lose his cool altogether. He often did."

"We're worrying ourselves about something that might, probably won't happen at all," Therese said. "He will stay in London, please God."

"When you start to bring God into it," Bridie almost laughed, "things really are in a sorry state."

"I suppose there are times when we do need some kind of power."

"If he was to do anything to Caomhán..." Bridie thought of the worst possible scenario as far as she was concerned.

"If he does come back you can get a court order to keep him away from you. If he breaks that he'll end up in Mountjoy."

"After he has me in the cemetery first. I'm afraid I don't find that there is much protection in the law. It's more on the side of men than women."

"You've been able to get away from him on account of the law. Wasn't it the law that put him in prison, that saved you from him for the past two years?"

Bridie wasn't impressed. "What good would that have been to me if he had killed me down the stairs?"

"Well, it wasn't the first time he'd hit you," Therese retorted. "Why didn't you report him before that?"

"Why didn't you report your father for what he was doing to you? Why don't you report him now?"

Therese had no answer to Bridie's logic. "You're right, Bridie. I know exactly what you mean. No matter how right it is, it's hard to turn in your father."

"I can tell you that it's even harder to report your husband. Especially if you're not yet eighteen years old and far away from home. Especially if you think you still love him."

"But you don't love him now, so things are different."

"He is still Caomhán's father. Oh, I wish life wasn't so complicated." On hearing his name, Caomhán brought over a pile of Lego he had put together.

"Isn't that lovely," Bridie said, even though there was neither head nor tail to it. "Show it to Teetie. To Therese," she corrected herself.

"Fair play to you." Therese told him he would be an architect. "That'd be far nicer than some of the things people I've asked for designs came up with. You'll be sure of a job with the Gaeltacht Board."

"Whatever you do," Bridie said to him, "be nice to your wife." She sometimes wondered if his father's genes would make him a batterer too. She worried aloud that being reared by two women might be bad for him in the long term.

"What harm could that do?"

"He might turn out gay, or something."

"What if he did? Most gay men I know are gentle and respectful to women. Why do men have to have this strut, this macho image? But I suppose the habits of centuries aren't changed overnight."

"I was so happy for the past couple of weeks," Bridie said, "I knew that something like this was bound to happen."

"Pishrogues, superstition." Therese shook her head, sounded as if she was disgusted. "I'll respect your faith, but spare me that old stupidity."

"It's always true all the same. When things are going any way well, you know you're due for a fall."

"Are you telling me your man was let out of prison just because you were feeling happy, and you needed to be taken down a peg? Another way to look at it is that it's not every day you get £500 in the post, free, gratis, and for nothing."

"That's why I can't keep it. There are strings attached."

"Put it into an account for Caomhán, and add anything else that you get from him. It will build up into a nice little nest-egg."

"I suppose you're right."

"Amn't I always?" Therese tried to lighten matters.

"A right ould shite," Bridie smiled, feeling a little better. "I could add his children's allowance to it every month." She was thinking out loud. "You'll soon be a rich little maneen." She hugged and kissed her son. He celebrated by breaking his Lego concoction into a hundred pieces, scattering them all over the floor.

Bridie felt the time passed very quickly from then until Christmas. She was decorating the house, setting up a Christmas tree, decorating it. She put a branch in a bucket of sand for Caomhán so that he could decorate his own tree. Anything coloured he found around the house, from soap to toilet paper, went on his little tree.

As the big day approached, Bridie brought

Caomhán with her on the bus to visit his grandfather and grandmother. It was there that the welcome and the presents awaited. Her father insisted that she bring Therese with them on Christmas Day for a visit. He tried to get Bridie and Caomhán to come for dinner. Bridie got out of that. She said they should have their Christmas dinner where they spent the rest of the year. "Anyway, we couldn't leave Therese to have dinner on her own."

"Hasn't she a family of her own to go to?"

"Her home is here in Connemara now."

"She must have some relations." The old man found it hard to believe that someone from as near as Mayo wouldn't go to her own people for Christmas dinner. "Or was it Santa Claus that brought her the first day?"

"She doesn't get on that well with her parents." Bridie felt that she had said too much, but it was too late to take it back now.

"Isn't she the strange sort of a woman too. You'd think that she'd have all the more reason to go home and make things up with them."

"She'll be welcome here for dinner as well as the two of you, if you want," her mother said. "We'll never eat a full turkey here between us."

"Therese doesn't like turkey."

"What will you be having if you don't have turkey?" The old man answered his own question. "A goose. I always thought that a goose was far more natural for Christmas dinner than a turkey." He spat into the ashes of the open fire. "It was always a goose that was in this house, when my poor father and mother, God be good to them, were alive. Then your mother came home from America with all her fancy notions." Bridie saw the twinkle of humour come to his eye. "A goose wasn't fancy enough for her. That was the time that the turkey was beginning to come into fashion."

"Which century was that now?" Bridie teased him.

"It's not that long ago at all, about a year before you were born."

Her mother winked at Bridie. "A turkey is nicer any day than that cantankerous old gander you had the first year that I was here. I was glad to see the last of him all right, he had the legs picked off me every time I went out to feed the fowl. He wasn't much of an adornment to the dinner table, though. There was more grease on him than meat."

"And good grease too." The old man warmed to his subject. "It was as good for the axle of a cart as it was for a woman's face. It was ten times better than that stuff ye do be getting out of little jareens in this day and age, trying to remove the marks of the years. There wasn't a woman with a wrinkle in her face while goose grease was being used on a regular basis," he said triumphantly.

"We could make our fortune if we started putting the grease of the goose in jareens," his wife joked, "and sold it within at the market in Galway of a Saturday morning along with the home-made jam and the cabbage and potatoes."

"Tell that to Thatch as an idea for the Gaeltacht crowd," he crowed. "There's women going around nowadays and they have lines on their faces like you would see on the trunk of a tree when you cut it. It's a great way of telling the years."

"Just as well some of the men don't look in the mirror too often." Bridie's mother gave her a conspiratorial wink.

"With a man you see what you get," he said. "With a woman you see what she'd like to see, no less and maybe a little more."

"We're having a duck for Christmas dinner," Bridie said when she stopped laughing at her father, "and scallops to start with."

"I wouldn't give a ten of clubs for a scallop." The old man spat contemptuously. "Famine food. That's what the people ate when they didn't have meat. People thought nothing of them until the French brought them into fashion. Any more than the turkey. An American thing. Why do we have to ape everyone? As for duck..." He shook his head resignedly. "Always aping. Aping everyone."

"That's what we should have," his wife was almost doubled over, laughing, "ape. There's a lot of that around."

"Well, Dad," his daughter told him, "we'll have the things that we like, and that's what we like, scallop and duck."

"And do you be eating at the same table as her ladyship?" Bridie didn't know whether he was serious or joking. She seldom did.

"Ladyship! You mean Therese? Sure she's the same as anyone else. She certainly doesn't boss me around."

"No one ever managed to boss you yet," Bridie was still the apple of his eye, "and I'm sure that no one will."

"Like father, like daughter," his wife joked.

"More like her mother," the old man said, "able to boss you without you knowing it." They were enjoying each other's company, Caomhán asleep on the sofa, the other members of the family still at school.

"I hear that John is out," her mother said quietly

after a while. Her father sucked at his pipe as if his mind was miles away.

"Where did you hear that?" Bridie was surprised.

"I met his mother in the village yesterday."

"He sent Caomhán £500."

"Where did he get that?"

"I don't know. There was just the cheque and a little note."

"So you know that he's coming home for Christmas?"

"He didn't say anything in the note, just to buy something for Caomhán."

"I hope he hasn't robbed a bank or anything," her mother said.

"I hope he has," Bridie answered her quickly. "and that he's caught and locked up for the rest of his life."

"He is your husband," her father, who hadn't seemed to be listening, reminded her.

"He was my husband. I'm not going back to him, whatever anyone says."

"For better, for worse." The old man spoke through teeth that held his pipe.

"For worse doesn't include nearly killing someone."

"He has his time put in, his debt paid, his lesson learned." Bridie's father was twenty years older than his wife. She often thought he sounded a hundred years older. Her mother came to her defence. "There are certain things that no woman can be expected to put up with. They put up with it in the past but not any more. But no one can stop him coming home and I suppose that he'll want to see his son."

"If he raises a hand to him..." Bridie didn't need to say more.

"His mother said that he's given up the drink."

"He's had plenty of practice at that. He gave it up at least twenty times while we were married. It never lasted too long, though."

"He told his mother that he's going to stay at home."

"Isn't it well that he could tell that much to his mother," Bridie said, haughtily, "and he couldn't tell his wife anything."

"Why would he, and her not writing or speaking to him for a couple of years?" The old man was as stubborn as ever.

"If you went through as much as I did with that man, Dad, you'd never speak to him again either. You have no idea what I went through with him. People who've had a soft life themselves don't understand these things."

"I hear people on the radio every day going on with that kind of talk," he answered her. "If they're not satisfied with the man they have, they get another in his place, like trading in a car. There's no talk of God, or of religion."

"A pity life isn't as simple as that," his wife cut him short. "Nobody knows how the shoe pinches the next person." She knew it was time to get away from serious subjects. She didn't want to send her daughter home depressed. "And what's Caomhán getting from Santa Claus? I couldn't ask until he fell asleep."

"It's a kind of clock that plays music when you twist a knob on it. But it has figures on it like a real clock. He'll be able to learn the time from it later. And he's getting paint and colouring pencils. And jigsaws. He loves jigsaws, and Therese is nearly as bad as him." Bridie looked at the presents her parents had bought.

"And all the things you got him, thanks again."

"They're not Santa stuff. He's seen them."

"Thanks for everything." Bridie gave a pretend kick to her father. "Even if you're always fighting with me."

"Tell that yellow-haired woman from me that she's welcome here any time," he said. "You mustn't be feeding her at all. The woman hasn't an inch of flesh on her. And I don't think that old duck is going to fatten her up much."

"Isn't it well that you be looking at the young ones, an old codger like you."

"She's an able dealer, that one," her father said admiringly. "I often hear her on the radio. She can give and take with the best of them."

"Isn't it lucky for you and the likes of you that has nothing to do but listen to that old radio all day," his wife joked.

"If Therese has her way he'll soon have Teilifís na Gaeltachta to watch all day as well," Bridie said.

"She's a fine woman," he said with genuine respect, "well able for any of that crowd that be trying to ask her trick questions on the radio."

"And better than most of them." Her mother winked at Bridie. "As you'd expect from a woman."

"They're better at talking all right," he agreed.

"You're a fair hand at the old chatter yourself," his daughter reminded him. "I'm looking forward to Caomhán being able to watch something in his own language by the time he starts at playschool."

"Life was a lot better before there was any television." The old man took the pipe from his mouth, before continuing. "People gathered around a big open fire to listen to a seanchaí. Sure there's no conversation at all now, everyone sitting around like zombies looking at a little box."

"You watch it yourself more than most, in case anything would happen in the world unknownst to you." His wife wasn't letting him away with anything.

"A man can't open his mouth in this house after six o'clock," he said directly to Bridie, "without your mother jumping down his throat for interrupting one of them, what do you call them? Soap operas. She's more interested in what happens in one of them programmes than in what the neighbours are doing down the road. Between you and me the same operas could do with a bit of soap, to clean them up."

"What is it but a pastime?" His wife dismissed the idea of soap operas being dirty programmes. "Sure isn't it a lot healthier to watch a nice story on the television than to be backbiting and discussing the neighbours' business? Wasn't that condemned by the catechism long ago?"

"It's a pity the catechism didn't know about soap operas or they'd have been condemned too. Pastime, how are you," he snorted. "Most of the time is passed doing something in public that should only be done by married couples in the privacy of their own bedrooms." He wasn't to be outdone.

"Get real, will you." His wife borrowed a phrase from her teenage children. "Sure we all know that these people on the TV aren't real, any more than Fionn and the Fianna that you'd have us hear about night after night are real."

"Fionn was an Irish warrior. And a gentleman. He didn't spend his time jumping in and out of other people's beds."

"Well, Diarmaid and Gráinne must have. Haven't

they a bed in every village in Ireland, stony old beds the most of them. Those great heroes of yours must have really known how to keep each other warm. It was a wonder they didn't end up with two slipped discs, the pair of them, on them rocky beds." Bridie enjoyed listening to them, each one giving as good as they got.

"Whatever it was they did or didn't do, nobody ever showed what they did in bed on television. That's my point." He smacked his lips in satisfaction.

"Sure they didn't have television, or they might have stayed at home and watched it." She deliberately misunderstood him. "It was worse to leave it to the imagination. I'd much prefer to spend a night watching television," she continued, "than to have to listen to some old *seanchaí* telling the same story night after night, getting angry with anyone that even stirred a foot to make themselves comfortable. I grew up with that kind of *seafóid*, and I had more than enough of it."

"Still, it must have helped to pass the long nights, before the telly was invented," said Bridie.

"I remember one night...." Her mother went on, "Old Pateen Tim beyond stuck his two fingers in the eyes of a young lad because he wasn't paying attention to him, even though the poor devil must have heard the same story a hundred times the same winter."

"Things were a lot better in the old days." The old man wasn't going to give in.

"How could things have been better, and us all living in poverty?"

"People were satisfied in themselves, and they had strong beliefs."

"They had, in fairies and ghosts, and superstitions. As for loving their neighbours... There wasn't a fair or a pattern or a dance that men didn't end up beating and killing each other. The young people of today don't do that. Well, most of them don't." She thought of her son-in-law at the last minute.

"They had no experience drinking," her husband said; "they didn't have the money to buy it. They worked hard and didn't have much to eat. It was no wonder that drink went to their heads."

"You've said it now, they didn't have enough to eat." She played her trump card with strong sarcasm. "As you say yourself, life was better then."

"Why is it that a woman always has the last word?"

"I didn't have the last word at all yet," she said.

"God help us when she gets going," he said and winked at Bridie.

"It's true for me." Mother spoke directly to daughter now. "I knew a woman that broke the handle of the brush on her daughter's back because the priest read her from the altar for being pregnant and single. Was that Christianity? The religion of being respectable was a lot stronger than the religion of Jesus Christ. And it still is. But I think your generation are going to have a lot more sense than we did."

"Only for the priests..." the old man tried to interrupt.

"Priests going around with blackthorn sticks, searching the ditches for courting couples. They'd have been better employed saying their prayers. No wonder the day came when there were no young women left to marry. They emigrated, and they were right. I was one of them myself. It wasn't for the money or for the high life that we went. We went because we were stifled at home." She paused for breath. The time for joking was over. She was angry now about the injustices of her youth.

"Only for the priests..." he began again, only to be interrupted.

"How many men were read from the altar down here?" Bridie's mother pointed in the direction of the chapel.

"There was no need to read the most of us, thank God," he said smugly, defusing his wife's anger at the same time.

"That's what you say now, you old goat," she laughed, remembering their own arranged but mostly happy marriage.

"Don't you know well that it was waiting for yourself to come back I was."

"I should have left you waiting."

They all turned around. Caomhán had woken up and began to cry in the unfamiliar surroundings. Bridie picked him up and he sat quietly on her knee for a while, his face red with sleep and teething. He pressed his head against his mother, looking from one to the other of his grandparents with big sleepy eyes.

He watched his grandfather puffing smoke from his pipe for a long time. Then he raised his hand suddenly and pointed, saying "Daideo", the Gaeltacht version of Grandad. This really pleased the old man.

"He's intelligent, but sure where would he leave it?" Caomhán's grandmother had put a little honey on a spoon and given it to him to help his teething. When he let the spoon drop after a few minutes, the little fellow said "Fuck." Bridie, reddened with embarrassment and pretended to ignore the word.

Caomhán pointed to the spoon on the floor and said even more clearly, "Fuck."

"As you say," his grandmother said to his

grandfather, "he's intelligent all right."

"He won't have much trouble learning his prayers," the old man added. His laughter took away Bridie's embarrassment. "He must think that's the word for a spoon." She looked at the old clock above the mantelpiece. "It's time I changed him and got him ready for the road. The bus'll be here in no time."

"It's a pity you don't have a while to spend with Susan and Johnny," her mother said. "They're out from school now and they'll just be coming off the bus when you are getting on it yourselves."

"They'll have plenty of time to play with him on Christmas Day." Bridie knew that they still treated their nephew as if he were some kind of elaborate toy.

Caomhán was angry when he saw his uncle and aunt get off the bus that he had to get on himself. He pulled and dragged, trying to follow them, but he soon settled down, pointing at animals in the fields, calling everything "*bóbó.*" Every animal was a cow as far as he was concerned.

Bridie felt comforted by her visit home. Whatever John might do, whatever was to happen between Therese and herself, she knew that she had the strength of her family behind her, that she could depend on them. They might be old-fashioned in many ways, they might spend half the time in fairly harmless arguments, but if you were in trouble you could depend on them one hundred per cent. And they were great crack. Smiling to herself she remembered some of the day's smart remarks, reminding herself, "I'll have to tell Therese about the goose-grease."

She felt sorry for Therese who had no contact with her parents. It was hard for her to even begin to understand what it was like to be abused as a child.

Even the battering she'd got from John hadn't been like that. She was a grown-up, able to call the police if she allowed herself. What could a child do when someone they loved betrayed their trust? Then suddenly she remembered that the woman she was feeling sorry for was probably having the time of her life at the Gaeltacht Board Christmas party.

At that very moment Therese was dancing a reel on top of one of the tables in the staff canteen, her audience cheering her on, jumping around and clapping hands to the music. Thatch was less drunk than most of them. Whatever else she'd do, she promised herself that she'd keep her head until she left the party. Too many people were only waiting for her to put her foot in it, to have an excuse to dismiss her. But there was no doubt where her staff stood. She was the hero of the hour.

Asked to sing, she gave a rousing rendition of "I'm Jake the peg, with me extra leg, diddel dee del didel dum," using a broomstick as her third leg. She then apologised for singing in English. "My only excuse," she said, "is that my extra leg has 'Made in Ireland' written on it."

She really brought down the house when she offered a prize to the first person onto the stage with "Made in Ireland" written on their extra leg. Like a stand-up comic in a bawdy bar, she began to tell a story:

"There was this famous Government minister, who will remain nameless, because you all know who he is anyway." Everyone cheered, knowing the joke, apocryphal or otherwise, was at the expense of their own Gaeltacht Minister, a man with a reputation, probably undeserved but greatly enjoyed by himself, for being "a big hit with the girls." Therese waited for the noise to die down before she continued:

"The great man was on his holidays in Greece a couple of years ago, one of those nudist beaches most of you have visited, I'm sure." Anything'd get a round of applause on the day, she thought, as she waited for the clapping to stop. "Someone beside him enquired was he from Newry, or had he been to New York. The reason for this was that the letters NY were tattooed on that extra leg we've been talking about." Another round of applause. "'It needs to be at full stretch to read it properly,' he said. 'Not New York. Not Newry. Newtown Mount Kennedy'." As the applause died down, Therese gave another twirl of the broomstick, "With me extra leg, didel dee, del didel dum."

When she had the audience's full attention, she switched from bawdy humour to a spirited talk on nationhood, language and culture, which she defined as practical patriotism. "It'll be some time," she told her fellow workers, "before I have you all together again as a captive audience, so I've a few more things to say if you will bear with me, a few messages to send to the powers that be." She took a drink of water, lowered her voice:

"You know as well as I do that there is a strong effort being made to subvert our plans for an independent self-financing Gaeltacht television station. You know that there are little yellow rags of newspapers trying to suggest that I'm trying to set up a private little television empire of my own." Pausing for breath, Thatch looked directly at her audience before continuing:

"I can tell you now that we're breaking no law,

supporting no party, putting no extra tax on anyone that isn't willing to pay it. We're creating something that is our right as inheritors of the culture and language of our fore-parents. We'll be providing high-tech, exciting, interesting jobs for the youth of the Gaeltacht. Anyone who doesn't want to be part of this can butt out. Any member of the Board especially who doesn't want to support us should have the guts to come out and say so. Anyone who doesn't want to be with us we'll do without. Happy Christmas."

Therese leapt down from the table and strode through the crowd, the ovation ringing in her ears. She sat into the Porsche, revved the engine, burned rubber in her take-off. She didn't go far, just in the gates of the hotel across the road from the offices. She could relax now. Most of the work-force would end up there sooner or later. She just wanted out of the offices before the *post mortem* on her speech would start. "I must have sounded like a little Hitler," she laughed to herself, "but I don't intend to take shit from anyone."

She stayed in the hotel bar until closing time. Knowing that she was well over her limit to drive, she asked one of the sober younger men, Tom Smith, a lorry driver who was a recovered alcoholic, to drop her home. She'd come back to collect her own car the following day.

Bridie left the sitting-room when Therese brought Tom in for a cup of coffee. "Three's a crowd," she said coldly when Therese followed her into the kitchen and asked her to join them.

"We'll just have a cup of coffee," Therese said.

"I thought my duties finished by midnight," Bridie said haughtily.

"Duties? What do you mean? I'm not keeping you up. I'm quite capable of making two cups of coffee myself. Tom will be away as soon as he's had his drink. Why don't you have a drink with us? It is Christmas."

"I have a child to look after in the morning."

"You have that to do every morning, and you often stay up later than this. What have I done on you this time?"

"Nothing."

"There's something wrong, or you wouldn't have a big puss like that on you."

"I have *not* a puss."

"Well, it's a very good imitation of one."

"If Peadar Halloran, or anyone else ever asks me out again," Bridie said, "I'm going out with them."

"Did I ever stop you from going out with anyone?"

"Did I say you did?" Bridie turned back at her room door. "Don't make too much noise, if you don't mind. The child is asleep."

There was a glint in Therese's eye as she said, "Don't worry, we'll be quiet, and discreet."

Therese's bedroom door was locked when Caomhán tried to go in to join her in bed the following morning, as he did nearly every day she was off work. She didn't get up until two o'clock in the afternoon.

"Caomhán and myself will be going home for Christmas dinner," was Bridie's greeting. "We were back there yesterday and they invited us."

"OK." Therese shrugged her shoulders, her eyes swollen-looking from sleep as she sat in her dressing-gown at the kitchen table. "It's a pity, though, that you didn't tell me sooner. I could've booked a place in one of those hotels that stay open for Christmas. It's probably too late now. Sure I'll be able to rustle something up for myself. I've always wanted to have just a boiled egg for Christmas dinner."

"I'm sure you will find some place suitable," Bridie said in a business-like manner.

"Why the sudden change? I thought you'd already bought the Christmas stuff, the duck, the booze, everything."

"We were getting on well at the time."

"And we're not now? What have I done, Bridie? It's far better to get it out in the open than to be going around moping about it."

"I'm not moping." Bridie spoke loudly through clenched teeth.

"There's no need to shout."

"I'm not shouting," she said, even louder.

"You're obviously upset about something."

"You locked out Caomhán this morning. I don't mind what you think of me, but please don't take things out on him."

"I didn't deliberately lock out Caomhán, but look at it from my point of view. Amn't I entitled to sleep out the first day of my holidays in my own house? I've been working very hard, and taking a lot of stick from journalists and politicians in the past few weeks. I'm just worn out."

"We all know how hard you work," Bridie said, sarcastically.

"You work just as hard, and if you want to sleep out any morning during the holidays, just ask me to mind Caomhán. I needed the sleep today, not that it seems to have done me much good. I feel more tired than if I was up at seven as usual. But that's beside the point. I know that's not the root of the problem. You had a face on you when we came back last night that would stop a clock."

"Well." Bridie shrugged her shoulders, not knowing what to say.

"Well, what?"

"Well, you brought home your fancy-man last night. When a man asked me out for the night, you weren't too pleased."

"Tom Smith, my fancy-man!" Therese had a great laugh. She explained about how much she'd had to drink, her fear not just of the breathalyser but of running someone down. "Anyway I never stopped you from going out with anyone. I'm not your mother. I don't care what you do with your private life."

"You could have minded Caomhán the night of the GAA social."

"I don't remember. Which night was that?"

"You'd think that it was jealous you were that I was asked out by a man."

"Just as I thought you were jealous last night," Therese replied.

"Me, jealous, of you and him!" Both burst out laughing together. Caomhán stretched out his hands to be taken up, to be part of the fun. They hugged him between them, swaying slightly in the middle of the floor.

"Maybe I was a bit rough on you the time that Halloran fellow asked you out," Therese admitted. "I must say I didn't like the idea of someone breaking up our own little family." She squeezed the two of them. "Sorry."

"It's all right."

"And I accept your apology too."

"For what?"

"For being such a bitch last night."

"Ah, F..." Bridie stopped herself in time. She laughingly told Therese of how Caomhán's language had embarrassed her in front of her mother and father the day before. "We'll have to be a bit more careful about what we say in front of him."

"You'd be as well to try and turn back the tide with a hay fork. There isn't a child in the world, never mind in Ireland that doesn't know that word." Therese snuggled her face against Caomhán's. "Aren't you the funny little man, letting down your Mammy in public."

"And how are things going to be now?" Bridie broke from the embrace, let Caomhán down gently to the floor, and sat down. "Will we allow each other to have friends? I don't mind really. I'm not mad to go out looking for a good time with a man, or anything. In fact I've sworn a hundred times that I'll never go out with one again. But if we've no other company than each other, we'll go out of our minds altogether."

"I agree, totally." The glint was back in Therese's eye. "So you didn't mind about Tom and myself last night?"

"Bang away for all I care. Even if he's young enough to be your son. You're old enough to have some sense."

"I'd want to have had him when I was ten years old if he was to be my son."

"Only joking."

"I'm glad I'm getting old," Therese said.

"I didn't mean that you are old." Bridie didn't want another row.

"Just that I look old. I must look like a real granny, at thirty-five."

"Nothing that a rub of goose-grease wouldn't cure." She told Therese about her father's recipe for eternal youth the previous day.

"He's probably right. I wouldn't be a bit surprised that if you'd some of the expensive stuff we buy analysed, there's nothing in them except what the old people used in days gone by."

"They probably never got spots or anything."

"A glass of their own every morning." Therese's eyes glinted with laughter.

"What do you mean, a glass of their own?"

"That's why they used to keep the potty under the bed. Where do you think the phrase 'taking the piss' originated?"

"You're the right piss-artist yourself." Bridie raised a fist in mock anger.

"Reminds me of a story."

"Another dirty one? Go on."

"There was this woman up in court for starting a row. The Justice asked her how it started. 'Well, it was like this, your honour. I was going to the doctor with a little jar in my hand. He'd asked me to bring in a sample. Your wan shouted across the street and asked me what was in the bottleen. "Urine," I said. "Your what?" she said back. "Urine," I said. "Your wine?" she said back. I knew she didn't understand me, so I said "Piss." That's when she got vexed and shouted "Shit" across the road at me. I went over and hit her a belt in the gob and told her to have a bit of manners'."

"Where do you get them?"

"When you're as old as I am you've a few tricks picked up along the way."

"I'll never live that one down," Bridie said. "You're not old, and you've done an awful lot with your life in a short time. You must be one of the most successful women in Ireland."

"I'd swap with you any time."

"You mean to say you'd like to be young again?"

"I would not. Will you go away with yourself. I'd hate it. Too many growing pains involved. It's because of Caomhán that I'd like to be in your shoes, as I've often said before."

"I never noticed that you liked nappies very much."

"I don't either, but he won't be in nappies much longer. In some ways he's at the hardest age to be minded just now. Full of curiosity. Into everything."

"Tell me about it." Bridie checked to see what he was at.

"But it's the nicest age in many ways. He's so full of love. He's lovely."

"Just like his mother."

"I set myself up for that one," Therese laughed, "but you're right."

"If we do stay another while, you'll have it both ways, the job and the child."

"So you might stay for Christmas?"

"You know me well enough by now, here today, gone tomorrow."

"You're about as sure of yourself as I am."

"I wish I was as sure of my future as you are."

"Let's take it a step at a time," Therese said. She went to her room, returned in a moment with an envelope which she gave to Caomhán. "This is from Mother Christmas; Father Christmas will be coming the next night."

"What is it?" Bridie asked. "Mind that he doesn't tear it." She took the envelope from Caomhán, opened it. Another cheque for £500. "Are you out of your mind?" she asked.

"I want to match his other father," Therese laughed.

"Put it in his account. It might come in useful some time."

"I can't accept this."

"It's not for you. It's for him."

"He's better off than his mother now. Caomhán, give a kiss to Teetie. Say 'ta-ta'." Therese kissed her on the mouth. "Happy Christmas."

"Happy Christmas." Bridie had her hand half way up to wipe her mouth to wipe off the kiss but she stopped herself in time. That would hurt Therese.

❧

John left Euston Station on the Friday before Christmas. Although he left the training centre early, he barely had time to have a shower, get dressed and take the Underground to Euston. As he queued for his ticket he had a good look around. It was a station famous in the history and folklore of Irish emigration. It was a noisy, happy, mixed sort of place that evening, thousands of Irish in the queues, the odd shout of "You'll never go back, Pat," ringing out over the buzz of many conversations.

A beautiful black girl sat into the seat across from him. He thought he'd start a conversation by cracking a joke. "Wouldn't you think it'd be a lot warmer at home in Africa at this time of the year?" She stood up, stared at him, and said icily, "I was born here, which is more than you were, Paddy." She almost spat the "Paddy" at him before moving to another seat.

"They don't know how to take a joke," he thought. Then he remembered that he wasn't too fond of the "Paddy" tag himself. He never took umbrage at it though, the way the coloured blokes would go bananas if you asked them, "When did you come down out of the trees?" He'd never said the likes of that to them, but he'd seen the swollen eyes and broken nose of the bloke that did.

"I'm on my way at last," he thought, although the train hadn't begun to move yet. But his course was set and barring accidents, rare on the railways, he'd reach his destination, that magic word marked on his ticket, "Galway." The City of the Tribes, tribes with fancy names like Ffrench with two "f's" as if someone long ago had a stammer when the schoolmaster asked them their name. He'd read about it years ago on the menu in Lydon House when his mother brought him in for a treat, tea and buns with coloured icing.

The only other tribe he could remember was Lynch. It was one of them who'd hanged his own son out the window when he was mayor of the city away back. Maybe it wasn't exactly out the window he'd been hanged. But John knew that the window built into the wall over beyond the big Protestant church had something to do with it.

"Some father," he thought, wondering would his own father have hanged him in circumstances like that. "He probably would and all." He remembered how strict his father was. He remembered him as a stern man who was especially contrary when he drank. It wasn't that he drank that much. He probably couldn't afford to. But when he went on a tear it was some tear.

An image came to John's mind from away back, him pissing in his pants as he waited for his father in the pub. The big sweaty men in the bar had a great laugh at the little puddle of water that formed in the sawdust around his red sandals with the six little slits on the front part of them. Even after his father died he'd never really forgiven him for that humiliation. It wasn't that he didn't love him, didn't miss him, but he hated him a little too. He wondered now had drink something to do with his early death from a heart attack.

No way would he treat his own son like that, he promised himself. That kind of a situation wouldn't arise anyway because he wouldn't be drinking. He hoped they'd be friends, man and boy playing football, working together on the bog and in the fields. He could see them doing a bit of carpentry like you would see Saint Joseph and the child Jesus in holy pictures, with Mary sweeping up the wood shavings. He hoped the young fellow would be good with his hands as he was. "Good with his feet too," he thought, thinking of the football.

As the train began to move he watched the late arrivals as they searched for seats. "Wouldn't I love to have that pair of legs wrapped around my arse." He was used to talking to himself by now, out loud as often as not, a prison habit. Too long on his own. He watched a tall young woman come up the aisle, legs to her arse as the lads used to say about mini-skirted girls. Strange how the mini had drifted in and out of fashion over the years. Since he'd left jail he sometimes thought they must have brought back the fashion just to drive him crazy with desire. "It won't be long now until I'm getting it regular," he thought of Bridie, "with the help of God."

"What's that, love?" An elderly woman was struggling to get into the place opposite him that the black woman had left. Looking at her shuffling into the seat John thought of the dog they had at home when he was a boy, turning and turning before sitting down. They had a joke about it, "One good turn deserves another."

"Just talking to myself," he told her good-humouredly, "and I couldn't be talking to a nicer person."

"A lovely Irish answer," she said. "I love the Irish." He was glad to meet someone that didn't seem to blame all the Irish for the latest bombing outrage. The old lady told him that she often went on a train journey just to hear Irish accents. She'd an Irish boyfriend at the time of the war. He'd disappeared, was presumed dead, after Dunkirk. She'd free travel now and would often take a train just to be among people, especially Irish people. She would take a return train from Crewe or Chester, or wherever the mood took her.

She kept talking, talking. John looked her straight in the face most of the time, trying to give the impression that he was listening. He was lost in his own thoughts much of the time, heard what she was saying at other times. He heard her saying that she didn't believe it when the tabloids said that all the Irish were animals. The Irishman she'd loved was the most gentle person that she'd ever met. She regretted now that they'd not been lovers, that she hadn't had his child. "But things were different then. He never laid a hand on me. Unfortunately," she said.

John tried to imagine her as a fresh-faced young woman in love. She must have been pretty then. He wondered had her Irishman been killed. Maybe he had deserted, returned to Ireland, raised a family. He was strongly tempted to tell her the man she loved was probably a grandfather back at home some place. It would be worth it just to see her reaction. Then he remembered the one-legged man in Piccadilly and he decided not to hurt her feelings. "I'll have to get out of that sort of crack," he told himself.

The old woman reminded John in some ways of his mother. He wondered what would she be like when he went home. Would she still be "ashamed of her life" as she'd told him when she visited the prison? He didn't really mind what she said to him. His attitude was that your mother was your mother, and it was natural for her to be giving out and trying to correct you.

He was finished with England. They had a nice place at home, his for the asking. The other brothers wouldn't come back from the States now that their children had started school. His sisters were settled down in Connemara and Galway. He had no doubt that his mother would give him the home place if he got his act together, brought back Bridie and the young fellow to live with him.

He was lost in a dream when the old lady stood up as they approached some station up past the English midlands. She'd get a return to London in an hour, "Just enough time to have some fish and chips and a bottle of pop." She said it had been lovely talking to him, that he'd reminded her of Bill. He was a credit to his family and his homeland, she told him before waving "Merry Christmas."

He wondered would he ever be so lonely that he would take a train just to be in people's company. But then the old dear had seemed quite composed and confident. She'd found a way to deal with her loneliness. It was a lot better than sitting at home moping. When he thought of it, his mother couldn't be compared to the other woman at all. She was out all day looking after her stock. Her daughters were all married around her. That was one advantage of big Irish families. "There's no place like the West," he told himself for the hundredth time, "no place like home."

It was very late when they reached Holyhead. There were queues there, as detectives did spot checks for drugs, sniffer dogs bustled busily around. They were still looking for the London bombers. One or two people were led away to an inner room, presumably for questioning. John felt that at least he couldn't look like a recently released convict. There was no attempt made to stop or question him.

The ferry was big and dirty, with a strong smell of vomit. "The crossing must be bad," John thought. He didn't mind, he had good sea-legs. He'd worked on one of the Aran Island ferries for a summer when he was a teenager. There was a long queue for tea and sandwiches. He joined it for a while, hoping he might recognise somebody, have a chat in Irish or in English, have some kind of communication with someone, anyone.

"Fuck this for a crack," he said when he saw how slow the service was. He went into the bar, but that disgusted him. Glasses had fallen from tables and there was beer all over the floor. A man lay in his own vomit, while a crowd of bearded bikers sang raucously, apparently they couldn't see the dirt and squalor around them. John reminded himself that the best day of his life was the day he gave up the drink.

He spent a while at the one-armed bandits, winning a handful of change with only his third pull. The greedy beast wasn't long in swallowing it all again.

John had enough sense to give up at that stage. He went out on deck as the ship headed into the Irish Sea. There was a stiff swell, and he amused himself for a while trying to balance himself on his sea-legs, rolling his feet to meet the waves, not holding on to anything.

He leaned on the rail then to watch the lights of Britain grow dim. A line of poetry from his schooldays crept through his mind, "Look thy last on all things lovely." As far as he was concerned the nicest part of England, even if it was Wales he was looking at, was leaving it. Back in the lounge he felt it strange that there should be so many people and so little talk, so little communication. He missed the old woman from the train. She might deafen you, but at least she tried to talk.

Imagination was the only cure for loneliness, as he learned in prison. On deck again he leaned on the rail and let his mind wander. He was teaching the young fellow—what the hell was it she'd called him?— to play football. He was about ten years old, stocky and muscular, more Bridie's build than his own. He went on a mazy solo run, left a couple of backs for dead and planted the ball in the back of the net.

While everyone else cheered and clapped and sang his praises John called him over to the sideline. He'd a quiet word with him about not being selfish when he was on the ball. He pointed out that another forward had been positioned for a pass, free on the left with a clear shot at goal.

"But didn't I score it myself, Dad?"

"You did, and fair play to you, but the backs could have fouled you, or pulled you down outside the square, and your team would've only a point instead of a goal. If the free was missed you'd have got nothing at all out of it. It's not the person that scores the goal that counts, but that it's scored."

How many hours had he passed like that in the last two years? It worked best with football and with women. That film he'd seen in Piccadilly had done the devil and all on him. You only had to think of it to get a hard-on. There was no way out of that other than working the hand, the left-hand ride as the Cockneys used to call it.

He'd many's the good night's sleep out of it since. "The landlady'll wonder how I starched the sheets so well," he thought. Not that it was half as good as the real thing. Bridie was better than most when she really let her hair down, he remembered. "I'm still madly in love with her." For one amusing moment he thought of wanking himself off over the side, a parting shot at receding Britain. "I'd do it too except that I'd probably end up getting my own back."

He laughed to himself as he remembered one of the Cockneys who claimed that a man thinks of sex every eight seconds. The same fellow gave the impression that it was every single second he thought of it himself. He often boasted of the latest wank he'd had, what he'd imagined, how long he'd held back the pleasure. That fellow had no shame at all in him but he was great gas. John had really liked him. He told himself that it was England he disliked, not the English.

Glancing at his watch he remembered that was the time the lads inside would be getting up, slopping out, lining up for the wash. He thought of the sour pork sausages and beans they'd have for breakfast, the sameness, the boredom, counting the days. Never again.

The ferry arrived in Dublin in the early morning. John decided to wait for an afternoon train. It would be too much of a rush to catch the connecting one. He was in no great hurry. Better to have a big breakfast first, savour the capital city for a couple of hours. Then he'd go west on a train that wouldn't be too crowded, as it wasn't meeting the mailboat buses. He was extremely hungry. He'd decided not to eat on the boat in case of seasickness. He looked around for a place to eat.

Wasn't it great to be back, a big Irish breakfast before you, bacon, eggs, sausages, black and white pudding, the *Irish Press* propped up against the bottle of YR sauce, a right paper without half-naked women sticking their tits into your eyes every page you turned. News and sport were matter-of-fact, not slanted by biased reporters. You'd know that you're home, he told himself.

He thought of buying something for his mother for Christmas. When he finished breakfast he strolled up O'Connell Street as far as Clerys. He bought her a warm woolly jumper. "Why didn't I think of this over yonder?" he asked himself. "I'd have got it for half the price." But you couldn't be mean at Christmas, not with your mother, especially. On a sudden impulse he bought a similar pullover for Bridie. "The Merc money won't last long at this rate," he told himself. " But it'll be worth it all if I can persuade herself and the little fellow to come back."

Wasn't it great to be alive, in your own country, looking up at the statue of the greatest of them all, Daniel O'Connell. John had admired him from his history classes. Looking further up the street he wondered who was the man with his arms stretched out in the air. He walked as far as the monument. James Larkin. He couldn't remember anything from school about him. A taximan idling beside his car at the end of the rank told him all about Larkin, praising him to the sky. "It must be because he was a bit of a communist that they didn't tell us about him," John said.

To pass a bit more time he went in to see the statue of Cú Chulainn in the GPO. "Bleeding to death because of an old bull or something," he tried to remember the story. As a west of Ireland man his own sympathies tended to be with Ferdia, but like so many Irish heroes, even Cú Chulainn seemed to be a loser in the long run. Cú Chulainn, Brian Bóramha, Eoghan Rua, even when they won they seemed to lose. History was one subject his old schoolmaster had loved to teach, passing on his passion to his pupils.

"Oh, Christ, I'm finished now anyways," was the first thought that struck him when two young nuns sat into the seat opposite him on the train. To his great surprise they pulled off the veil things from their heads, took out a pack of cards and asked him did he want a game. Was he able to play twenty-five? What a pity he hadn't company like that on the train and boat the night before, he thought, "I wouldn't have been bored out of my mind."

There was great crack in the two nuns and they didn't mind cheating at cards. They discussed the men who went up and down the train like any young women would. John thought that they were like young fillies let loose in a field for the first time, airy and excitable, a joy to be with. When the trolley came around he stood them scones and coffee. "You'll be able to tell everyone when you go home that you had two nuns and a bun for tea on the train," one of them said. They had a great laugh at that. "Isn't it grand to be innocent too," he said to himself.

They'd be with him as far as Athenry, they told him, when he said that he was going to the end of the line. They'd just spent three months on a course in St Patrick's College, Maynooth, and were going back to their mother house for the Christmas.

"I didn't realise you were sisters." He thought they'd said "mother's house." This led to all kinds of puns on "sister" and "mother." "Our ould Ma's at home are a lot more reverent than the Reverend Mother," one of them said.

"But the mother we have in Maynooth is a right bitch," the other nun added.

"I thought Maynooth was for priests," John said. "Are they letting women join at last?" He wouldn't have been a bit surprised. Anything might have happened unknown to him while he was inside.

"A pity that they're not," one of the nuns laughed. "Thousands study there now," she explained, "as well as students for the priesthood."

"I'd have gone to Maynooth myself," he joked, "if I thought that they'd the likes of the two of you there."

They asked him every kind of a question. Had he a girlfriend? Was she nice? Did he intend to marry her? He answered them as truthfully as he could without letting himself down in front of them. He said that he loved a girl back home and was looking forward to spending the rest of his life with her.

He didn't mention the child. They mightn't have much understanding of that kind of thing. They seemed innocent in spite of acting like women of the world. "There'll never be an end to religion," he complimented them as the train approached Athenry, "as long as the Church has women like the two of you working for it." He helped them with their bags and went back to his seat. There they were knocking at the window, throwing kisses at them. "The brazen hussies," he thought affectionately. He blew kisses back at them as the train moved off. "The mad bitches."

He stood at the train window from there to Galway, looking out at the great stretches of green fields, the area known west of Galway as the *eachréidh*. How many spalpeens from his part of the country had come there, spade on shoulder, to look for seasonal work? There were some good houses but most of the men had been billeted in sheds and in lofts, almost slaves, like the American blacks. But the day had come that the Connies, as Connemara men were known, were as good as anybody. The best housing in the country was west of the Corrib nowadays.

After twenty-four hours' travelling he was at last on the platform of Galway station breathing the air of home. The smell of Galway mixed with the smell of Christmas. He walked around Eyre Square to soak in the atmosphere through every pore. It was great to be alive and in Ireland. Home at last.

His mother gave him a great welcome when the taxi pulled up outside. It wasn't as good as coming in the Mercedes, but so what? She had a lovely tea prepared. There was no mention of prison; you'd think he'd never been inside. Two of his sisters visited later but didn't stay long. They knew how tired he'd be after the journey, having done it many times themselves in days gone by. They promised that they'd bring the children around to see him when he was well rested.

His mother offered him a night-cap, but he refused. He boasted that he hadn't touched a drop for almost two years. He'd never touch it again, he promised. He could see the joy in her eyes.

"Maybe you'll stay at home altogether this time."

"That's what I have in mind, if it's all right with you."

"Of course it is. I'm getting too old to be running around after cattle."

"I was never a great man for the land myself," John said, "but I could be working in the city or some place, and have a few store cattle on the land."

"Cattle are going a great price at the moment," his mother said.

But John wanted to work on buildings or in a factory. "Is there much work about?" he asked.

"The Gaeltacht Board is providing a lot of work in the last couple of years. There's a great little woman at the head of it now. She's really got things humming. Bridie's working for her."

"Is she working in an office?"

"No, she's running that woman's house for her."

"She must have a very big house."

"She works very hard; the least she might expect is to have her dinner ready when she comes home from work in the evening. Not that she goes home that often, she's often out in the pub until all hours, dancing sets and everything just like one of the girls."

John misunderstood. "Bridie?" he asked.

"No, Thatch, as they call her. How could Bridie be out, with a baby to mind?"

"I'm dying to see the young fellow."

"Isn't it you that was silly too?"

"That's all water under the bridge now. I haven't

had a drink in two years," he reminded her again. "I'm willing to put in a good day's work wherever I get it. I've learned my lesson."

"I know you have, but what's Bridie going to do?"

"I don't mind if she wants to stay working for your woman. If we're to build a house, we'll need the extra salary."

"That's not what I'm saying. Maybe she won't want to go back to you."

"She'll come around all right," John said confidently. "I sent her £500 the other day."

"Where did you get £500? I hope you didn't get into bad company in that place."

"Do you remember that nice car I had the last time? The lads sold it for me and put the money in the bank."

"I saw him in the chapel a while ago, the little lad. He's lovely, the picture of yourself when you were that age. And just as bold," she laughed. "He had the priest driven half crackers. He hates to hear children making a racket."

"Some things never change." John remembered the old PP.

"It's hard to blame him. He suffers a bit from the nerves."

"Yeah," he said slyly, "when we were serving Mass we thought it was because of the altar wine that he always smelt of drink."

"Bridie's mother told me the last day that she can't bring him to Mass any more until he's a bit bigger."

"She must have him spoiled."

"They're all the same at that age. You were worse, except that we had a nice priest at the time. He used to say that the cry of the child was nearer to God than the prayers of all the rest of the people in the chapel."

"What would be the best time to go and see them?"

"It's hard to say. She could hardly turn you away from the door at Christmas."

"He's my son. I must have rights."

"You wouldn't know how she'd be. Women have got very uppity in recent times. They'll tell you up straight about rights, their own rights."

"She's hardly one of them feminists."

"The one she's working for certainly is. I often hear her on the radio; nothing for her but equality of the sexes as she calls it."

"I'm sure Bridie isn't into stuff like that. She's hardly changed that much in a couple of years."

"Women are a lot bolder now than they were in my time."

John didn't know whether that was praise or condemnation. "When she sees how much I've changed..."

"Sleep on it," his mother said. "Your eyes are beginning to close."

Tired and all as he was, John found it hard to sleep. The noise of the train rattled in his head. People moving, talking, lights flashing by, the rise and fall of the boat. It was as if his journey home had come back to haunt him. It was on an occasion like that a man could do with a drink. But that was no longer open to him.

Could Bridie really reject him after all he'd been through? he asked himself. Had his mother got some kind of a hint? After much tossing and turning he concentrated on the film he'd seen in Piccadilly. With himself and the two nuns from the train in place of the actors, he satisfied himself quickly with his hand. He fell asleep immediately after that.

❧

Christmas Eve was cold and wintry, with a harsh north-east wind blowing occasional showers of hailstones. Therese had spent most of the morning in bed while Caomhán climbed all over her. Bridie sang to herself in the kitchen as she prepared potatoes and vegetables for the big day. She wanted to have as little housework as possible to do on Christmas Day. She'd just put the duck in the oven for a couple of hours and do the rest in the half hour before dinner.

She'd already cleaned the scallops and put them back in their shells with onion and grilled rashers before covering them with mashed potatoes. They'd have half a dozen on Christmas Eve and the other six as a starter on the following day. She was enjoying herself. This was the first time she'd prepared the festive dinner on her own.

She brought tea and toast to the others in bed, though she well knew that Caomhán would have crumbs all over the place. Things like that never upset Therese. "Never mind," she said as Bridie fussed, "it's me that has to sleep in it."

As they sat there the telephone rang beside Therese's bed. She picked it up, listened for a moment. "Hold on." She handed the receiver to Bridie. It was John. She panicked. "I can't talk to you now," she said. "I'm very busy. The house is full of people, people from the Gaeltacht Board," she lied. "There's an important meeting going on here, something to do with the new television station." She didn't know what to say.

"I won't be a second," he said. "I just want to make

arrangements to see the young lad soon."

"Call me after Christmas," she said, and put down the phone. She was shaking. "I had to say something," she explained to Therese. "I was lost for words."

"You'll have to face him some time," Therese said quietly.

"I don't even want to think of him until after Christmas. I want this to be a happy Christmas for the three of us, especially if it's the only one we'll have together. I want to be happy and merry as well and fuck the begrudgers."

"That's the stuff," Therese said. "There's nothing like a positive attitude."

"I got such a surprise when he rang. I was all up in a heap."

"The important meeting was a good one."

"I had to say something."

"I think it was a great idea." Therese was as supportive as she could be. "The more people he thinks are coming and going in and out of this house the better. He'll be less likely to try something on."

"His voice hasn't changed one bit," Bridie said amazed. "You'd think it was yesterday I was talking to him last."

"At least he was civil, wasn't he?"

"He never asked me how I was or anything."

"Between you and me, you didn't give him much time."

"I suppose I bit the head off him really."

"You were just right," Therese reassured her. "He caught you off your guard. You'll be expecting to hear from him from now on. It'll be different. You'll have something ready to say when he calls."

"What would you say to him, Therese, if you were

in my shoes?"

"I'd be as matter-of-fact as anything. I'd have a plan in my mind. Tell him he can see Caomhán for four or five hours a couple of times a week."

"That'd be for too long altogether."

"I'm just giving my opinion," Therese said crossly. "You did ask me what I'd do if I was in your shoes."

"You're right. I'm sorry. But five hours!"

"Four, three, two, one. Whatever you decide. You can call the shots here, Bridie. He comes into this house at your invitation. It's you that calls the tune. If you think five hours too long, if you think twice a week's too often, that's fine. Just have a definite time and place. Have a deadline that he has to stick to, or he can forget about it."

"I think once a week is plenty for a start."

"That's my girl. That's the way to do it. Call the shots. Lay down the law."

"What about four hours?" Bridie answered her own question. "Sure he could have him kidnapped or anything in four hours."

"Three?"

"Three hours is a long time."

"What about two for a start? See how he behaves himself. You can allow more after that if he earns it, if he deserves it."

"Two hours once a week. God, I feel awful mean."

"See how he reacts to that first, Bridie. You can use it as a bargaining position or anything then. You're in charge on this one. Never forget that."

"I know now why they say you're a tough cookie."

"We women need to be tough." Thatch clenched her fists, giving two thumbs-up signs at the same time. "It's a man's world." She smiled. "Well, it used to be."

"Would you like more toast or anything?"

"Mammy, Mammy." Caomhán raised up the bedclothes so that his mother could get in beside himself and Thatch.

"That settles that," she said. "You'll see to it that your old mother will get to rest her weary limbs anyway." She lay down. He settled down to suck his thumb and cuddle his teddy bear between the two women. They began to remember past Christmases, good and not so good.

"The funniest one I remember," Bridie said, "was the year there was no price at all for the turkeys so we had to eat most of them ourselves. As I was a good few years older than the other two, needless to say I ended up having to do a lot of the plucking. All I remember is broken nails and tough feathers. Between that and the same thing for dinner week after week, it's no wonder that I don't want to see a turkey again. I certainly don't want to pluck one or any other kind of a bird for that matter."

"I'm not a pheasant plucker." Therese quoted the old rhyme used in more daring elocution classes. They both ended up with more "pleasant fuckers" than "pheasant pluckers" as they tried to say it quickly. Caomhán knew that this word was always good for a laugh, so he said "fugger" as often as he could, to the delight of the grownups.

Therese had memories of some good Christmases before her father began to abuse her and her mother became permanently ill. The thoughts made her sad. "Let's just live for today, and tomorrow," she said. "Forget painful pasts."

They spent a couple of hours in the pub in the afternoon, leaving when Caomhán got particularly rowdy and noisy. After one man had given him a pound he started to go from person to person, his hand out for money. Bridie was so embarrassed when she noticed this that she tried to give the money back. The men laughed good-naturedly, saying, "Isn't it Christmas?"

Therese took care of Caomhán while Bridie was at midnight Mass. Bridie enjoyed the atmosphere, the singing and the music. Afterwards she went down on her knees at the crib. She thanked God that things had worked out so well for herself and Caomhán. She prayed that John's return wouldn't lead to upset or trouble. She began to giggle when the figure of Joseph reminded her of Therese, who seemed to have the same role in their "family."

They went to bed reasonably early, knowing that Caomhán would be awake at cock-crow. He'd heard so much about Santa Claus by now that he seemed to understand that there was going to be a big surprise for him in the morning. Therese asked to be called if she wasn't awake in the morning. She didn't know about religion, she said, but she'd always liked Christmas.

Therese said she wouldn't enjoy the celebrations if she wasn't at some religious service. "Call it nostalgia, call it a very weak faith, call it cultural conditioning, call it anything you like, Christmas would not be Christmas without church. It'd be like going to a wedding reception after skipping the wedding. I'd feel guilty about it." She explained that in London she used to go from church to chapel, Catholic, Protestant. She used to love the hymns when she was lonely and far from home.

"You needn't apologise for it," Bridie said. "I know that you're a very spiritual person at the back of it all."

"At the back of it all. That's a backhanded compliment if I ever heard one."

"I don't mean it like that, just that your heart's in the right place."

"You think you'll convert me yet."

"I don't need to. You're the best person I ever met."

"Bullshit," Therese said, embarrassed by such praise. "Cut the crap, and let's get on with organising this Santa Claus stuff or he'll get up and find these two old Santies wrapping presents at the last minute."

As expected, Caomhán was awake early, tearing wrapping paper and scattering it in all directions. Bridie showed him how to get music from his clock. There was no point in trying to keep him from wakening Therese until it was time to get up. He had to show her his present. The three of them sat in her bed opening presents from each other, chattering and joking. Therese insisted on getting Bridie's breakfast.

"Lie back there. It's the least I might do one day in the year."

Bridie felt like a queen, lying back on the pillows, sipping the glass of brandy Therese brought in for her while she was grilling rashers, sausages and black pudding as well as her first attempt at poached eggs. Bridie's biggest fear was that Therese would burn the bottom out of the saucepan. "Not to worry," she thought, "isn't it her own. She has plenty of money to buy another if it's needed. Relax, woman. Enjoy it while you have it." She snuggled down in the bed. "I could get a taste for this," she shouted out towards the kitchen.

"This is strictly a once-off," Thatch joked. "I'm afraid there'll be nothing but bottomless saucepans by the time I've finished."

Therese was still at Mass when the sound of Caomhán crying woke Bridie, who'd fallen asleep after the brandy and the big breakfast. She got a shock when she went into the sitting-room and saw him, blood running down his forehead into his eyes. He'd hit his head on the coffee table as he bent to pick up one of his new toys.

The cries were worse than the cut. The skin was broken just below the hairline. "You'll be all right before you get married," she said as she washed and bandaged him in the bathroom. She wound a bandage around his head to prevent him bumping the cut again. He was very proud of himself when she showed him his reflection in the mirror. He laughed and pointed at the bandage with his finger.

"How am I going to clean the carpet?" was the next question, but she wasn't really worried. A new one could be bought from his thousand pounds if it came to that. The main thing as far as she was concerned was that Caomhán was all right. She managed to clean up completely without leaving a mark because the blood was so fresh. She took her son in her arms and they sat in a big soft armchair as he sucked his thumb and pressed himself against her. "So much for brandy." Once again she reminded herself, "You can never let a child out of your sight."

They visited Bridie's parents about midday. They were asked to eat at least the turkey giblets, because, as her mother said, "It wouldn't be Christmas at all without some turkey."

Susan and Johnny were allowed to bring Caomhán to the neighbours' houses on condition that one held each hand and that they'd make sure that he didn't fall again. He came back with a pocketful of money.

"You have him well-trained," her father told Bridie.

"It's so embarrassing." She told him about his collection in the pub the previous day. "You can't take your eyes off him for a minute."

"Ask your Daideo for money, Caomhán." Therese enjoyed slagging the old man. "We'll soon find out how well-trained he is."

Caomhán held out his hand. His grandfather spat on his own hand and gave a little slap to Caomhán's, like a jobber at a fair.

"That's it, teach him more bad habits," Bridie said.

"He has to learn to make a bargain, or he won't get anywhere in life. You'd think he'd have learned that much from the businesswoman there." He took a pound coin from his pocket. "You'll get the money if you do this." Sure enough Caomhán imitated him, spat on his little hand and smacked his grandfather's as hard as he could. He laughed uproariously as he did so again and again.

"That's the best Christmas present I could give him," the old man winked at Therese, "show him how a man makes a bargain." He was hoping to draw her into some feminist reaction so that they could have a good rousing argument, but she didn't budge.

"You're getting a bit long in the tooth now for winking at the girls." His wife was passing around generous helpings of her huge old-fashioned Christmas cake.

"A man never gets too old for the good things of life. Sure isn't it natural," a word he pronounced in the country fashion "nackeral."

"Knackered might be a better description for some people I know," she shot back a good-natured barb.

"It's all in the mind," he said.

"So I've noticed."

The younger people were in stitches laughing at them as they ping-ponged puns across the open fireplace. Therese, as an outsider in the Gaeltacht, was always amazed by the ease with which sexual innuendo was used among older people especially, people who were often quite conservative in other areas of life. She had heard it said that it was because Jansenism, that brand of French Catholic Puritanism, rife at the time Maynooth College was founded, had never got a grip in the Gaelic speaking areas. The preachers were probably not good enough at speaking the language to have their message understood. Or maybe their listeners didn't want to hear. She often used this notion of a freer language in public debates as yet another reason for the revival of Irish.

The day was getting on. Greetings, blessings, well wishes for Christmas, the New Year, "and many of them," were exchanged. *"Nollaig shona agus Athbhliain faoi mhaise"* rang in their ears as Therese, Caomhán and Bridie got into the car. Susan and Johnny made faces through the windows at their nephew as the Porsche eased out towards the front gate.

They had a walk on the beach on their way home to give them an appetite for their dinner. They sat down to their meal at about five. There were candles lighting on the table, classical music in the background, champagne, red and white wines, food, followed by Gaelic coffees made with poteen. They decided that they were too full for dessert and left the Christmas pudding for another day.

They watched television until it was time to put Caomhán to bed. They didn't know what to do with themselves then. "It's true what they say," Bridie said.

"Christmas is really for children. There's nothing for grown-ups to do but drink."

"We could have a worse complaint."

"It's tomorrow morning I'm afraid of. After the last time we had a right tear. I swore I'd never let it happen again. It's not worth it."

"It's different though when you have a good feed inside you," Therese said. "Speaking from experience and all that."

"It just gives you more to throw up."

"Could we change the subject?" Therese was laughing at the idea. "A bit more talk like that and you'll have me retching."

"Feel free," Bridie joked. "It didn't stain the carpet the last time."

"Why don't we dance?" Therese asked. She put on some modern music and they danced until Bridie flopped down on the sofa, exhausted. Therese changed the tempo, put on an old Perry Como waltz and stretched out her hands for Therese.

They danced very slowly, very closely, hardly moving from where they stood. They could feel an excitement in each other. When the kiss came it was natural and long. They stood for a long time, cheek to cheek, as if holding each other up, afraid to move in case the moment would be lost. At last Therese broke away, put the fireguard to the chimney, checked that the doors were locked, knocked off the lights. Bridie followed her to her bedroom.

"This isn't right."

"Just lie beside me and put your arms around me. That's all. What's wrong with that?" Therese asked.

Caomhán was delighted the following morning to find them in the same bed. He climbed in between them. Bridie suddenly screamed when he put a cold hand on her. "You're like ice!" They cuddled, played with and tickled him for a while until he settled down between them, wanting to sleep.

"You wanted more than that, didn't you?" Bridie was looking down at Caomhán sucking his thumb. She was afraid to look Therese in the face.

"Are you mad with me?"

Bridie shrugged. "That's your business."

"That's the only way I can love. Another woman."

"Don't be saying things like that."

"It's true, for me."

"I don't want to hear it."

"I can't pretend that I'm otherwise."

"Look," Bridie felt her face redden with embarrassment, "this life probably suits both of us. You're like a second mother to Caomhán. I know that we both had our troubles with men, but I'm no lesbian."

"I know you're not," Therese said, "and I don't want any more complications than you do. Christmas is such a lonely time. I just needed a cuddle, an arm around me. That's all."

Bridie wanted to talk about it. "I could have objected. I didn't. I suppose I needed a bit of warmth too. It's a night people want to be, I suppose, great with each other. Things go too far. But love, that's something else. I like you. You're good to me, to Caomhán. But I'm no lesbian. I've nothing against someone who is but I'm not like that. It's not my nature. I like men, even though I've had a very bad experience with one of them." She shrugged. "I don't know what I'm trying to say."

"I like men too. I don't know what lesbian means.

I know what the word means, but as for feeling like that... Maybe I'm bisexual, who knows? I don't feel attracted to women more than men, but I love you more than anyone I've ever met, woman or man. That's what I was trying to show you last night without doing anything about it, if you know what I mean..."

"It's not right," Bridie insisted. "I'm not saying that it couldn't happen. I just know that it's not right."

"I find nothing wrong with it. Do you mean the very idea of it makes you feel dirty?"

"It's not that. I just feel that it's wrong. That's all."

"Because of your faith, religion, or whatever?"

"Maybe. I don't know. Whatever the Church says, I don't think God would object to people having a bit of satisfaction if it doesn't harm anyone else. But that's not it. It's something deeper than that, something that goes to the bottom of my being. It's not right for me. It's not natural for me, but I could understand that it would be to someone else."

"I don't see it as satisfying natural urges, even though that's part of it. I see it as a way of showing love," said Therese.

"That kind of talk embarrasses me. I don't know what love is."

"You know what love is better than I do. You know what you feel for Caomhán."

"If that's the way, then this certainly isn't the same thing." Bridie continued, "The love you have for your child is different anyway from love of a grown-up, whether it's a husband or a parent, or whatever. I don't know." She sat up suddenly. "That's the doorbell."

"Leave it," Therese said, "I'm sure it's only the wren boys. Let them come back later if they're that badly off for money. You'd think their parents wouldn't let them out so early on a holiday morning."

"I'd bet that their fathers and mothers are still asleep, it's just that the young ones don't have hangovers after Christmas Day. And it's a chance for them to make a bit of pocket money."

"It's easy to see which of us is the mother," Therese said.

Bridie tickled Caomhán. "Won't you be going around on the wran in a few years, collecting money for your mammy?" He smiled at her, enjoying the attention even though he didn't know what she was talking about.

"Discrimination again," Therese said. "Why is it only boys that be out today?"

"The girls have their day on the first of February. I used to make my fortune on the Brídíní. It's a pity I'm too big to go out on it this year," Bridie joked.

"The two of us should do it for the crack."

"I think we're a bit long in the tooth," Bridie said, baring her teeth at Caomhán, "some longer than others."

"Don't remind me."

Bridie suddenly got serious. She asked Therese, "Would you mind answering the doorbell if anybody rings in the next couple of days?"

"In case John comes around? I don't mind, but you know you have to let him meet Caomhán some time."

"I'm not ready for that yet, but before he goes back."

"Is he going back?"

"I hope to Christ he is. How will I keep him away from me if he isn't?"

"Get a court order if he tries anything on."

"I'll kill him if he lays a hand on Caomhán," Bridie said nervously. "What if he tries to take him, kidnap him?"

"You're thinking of the worst possible things that can happen. He'll know that if he does anything foolish he'll never be allowed see his son again. But give him a chance; maybe prison has made him grow up."

"I know John."

"Anything you need—money for a solicitor or anything like that—I'll look after," Therese promised.

"Ah, you're very good."

"And Bridie," Therese looked her in the eye, "I'm not going to try anything on with you, take advantage of you..."

"I should think not." Bridie raised a fist, half serious, half mocking.

"Sex would be as big a threat to me as it is to you right now."

"How do you mean a threat? Well, that kind of sex would, the kind we were talking about. You're right about that."

"I think myself that sex fucks up a relationship."

"Literally, and in more ways than one."

"I'm serious, Bridie. I think that what the two of us need is a bit of support, emotional support."

"I could do with a big hunk with a hairy chest right now." Bridie was feeling too giddy for serious conversation. "That's the kind of support I'd like."

"I'm sorry about that. I can't supply the hairy chest anyway. I'm sure there are plenty of men around that would oblige at the drop of a hat."

"At the drop of a pair of pants, actually."

"Well, what's stopping you?"

"To tell you the truth, I couldn't care less if I never saw a man again. It's an overrated pastime anyway."

"Looking at men?" Therese teased her.

"The other. You pays for your pleasure."

"Isn't that what I'm trying to say, that emotional support is far more important."

"Except when you feel like having a good fuck."

"Fuck." Caomhán picked up on the laugh word again.

"That fellow has it on the brain already," Bridie laughed.

"Where would he leave it?"

"It was you was the randy one last night."

"I beg your pardon."

"It was obvious, the way you danced."

"Don't confuse sensuality with, with whatever."

"Oh, no. You're lovely when you're acting the holy innocent."

"Amn't I lovely anyway." Therese preened herself.

"There's nothing wrong with fancying yourself."

"I couldn't fancy a nicer person."

"John used to say something like that."

"Speaking of which, when have you decided to let Caomhán see him?"

"Would you like to meet your Daddy?" Bridie asked her son.

"Daideo." He smiled when he thought of his grandfather.

"He doesn't know what 'Daddy' means," Therese said.

"The way things are around here at the moment," Bridie laughed, "I suppose that he thinks that you're his Daddy."

"At least you haven't lost your sense of humour.

You're as giddy as anything today."

"If we can't laugh we'd be as well to be dead." Bridie settled herself comfortably in the bed. But Therese jumped out on the floor, full of beans.

"Let's go," she said. "Stephen's Day is always a great day in the pub."

"This time of the morning? Are you out of your mind, woman? Didn't we drink enough yesterday to do us for another year?"

"I'm going anyway. There'll be great music, wrenboys and everything."

"Caomhán will embarrass me again, collecting from everybody."

"Not a bad trade at all. You'll make a priest out of him yet. All he'll have to do is pass around a basket to make a bit of money," Therese slagged. "Come on out of that. If he gets tired or contrary we'll come home."

"You can drop us back here so, if he gets rowdy," Bridie said, "and go back again yourself."

"Don't be daft. I want to be where you are."

"Don't start that soppy old stuff again."

"It's true. Come on and we'll have a shower."

"Carry on. Caomhán and I will have ours after you."

"We'd be quicker all together."

"Water isn't that scarce."

"Don't be such an old *cailleach*."

Bridie carried Caomhán with her and skipped into the shower when she knew that the water was good and hot. The little fellow had a great time. Wrapping a towel around herself, Therese said, "Human nature, why should it embarrass us?"

"Yourself and your nature." Bridie threw a handful of water at her. "Too much nature we're having if you ask me." Caomhán joined in the fun, throwing water until the bathroom was drenched.

"Stop, stop, stop," his mother said. "I suppose I can't blame him. I started it myself."

It was midday before they had breakfast finished and headed for the pub. There was a good crowd there even at that time. It was as if the pub closure of the previous day had been some terrible imposition on the drinking public, and there was a lot of catching up to be done.

They'd missed the small wrenboys, schoolboys going from house to house, by not staying at home. But they didn't miss the bigger ones, groups of men in ragged clothes and masks, some made of straw, musicians, *sean-nós* singers, dancers, hangers-on, going from pub to pub.

Caomhán was frightened at first of these strange-looking beings, but when he saw his mother and Therese laugh at them he knew that there was no threat. He began to clap his hands to the music and jump up and down, trying to dance.

One of the wrenboys whisked Bridie out in a set. There was something so familiar about his style of dancing that she knew that she should recognise him. Peadar Halloran? But he was taller than Peadar. Maybe he had high-heeled shoes.

"You never lost it," he said, "the dancing." She immediately recognised his voice.

"John!" They stood in the middle of the floor, the dance going on around them. "Isn't he lovely," he said, looking at Caomhán. "His daddy's picture," he joked. Bridie tried to hide her nervousness, to be businesslike:

"You can see him if you come to the house

tomorrow between three and five." She remembered
what she and Therese had decided earlier, be specific,
be definite. Bridie thought it safer to be on home
ground and Therese wouldn't be far away. "We can
arrange future visits at that stage."

"I never thought that I'd have to make an
appointment with my wife in order to be able to see
my son."

"You wouldn't either, if you hadn't nearly beaten
her to death." Bridie didn't put a tooth on it, knowing
that now was the time to lay down ground rules. "Take
that thing off," she said about the mask, "it's like
trying to talk to a statue." They moved aside from the
dance floor. "If you want to see Caomhán regularly,
it'll have to be on my terms," she said. "I don't want
him upset every time you visit. Some kind of a rag-doll
being tossed back and over between the two of us."

"There's no need to come the heavy on me, Bridie."

"To tell you the truth, I'd have preferred if you
hadn't come back, but I suppose when he has a
father..."

"Don't be so hard on me, Bridie. I've changed
completely."

"How often did you change completely before?"

"I haven't had a drink in two years."

"I didn't expect they'd have lounge bars in prison,"
was Bridie's scathingly sarcastic reply.

"I'm out of there for ten weeks. There was plenty of
temptation to go on the batter, but I didn't give in to
it."

"I'll believe it when I see it."

"Even today it's me that's driving the lads. I'm the
only one on the wagon, the only one of them that's
not drinking."

"Three to five, tomorrow." Bridie wanted to keep a distance. She left him and sat down beside Therese, who had Caomhán on her knee. "I'd like to go home soon," she whispered.

"Is that him? Well, the ice is broken now anyway."

"Not this iceberg, it hasn't. But for Caomhán's sake..." They finished their drinks and left. On their way home they had a long walk in silence on the bog road before lighting a fire early. They watched television all evening. Both women were lost in their own thoughts most of the time.

Bridie slept little that night. She was full of nerves about John's visit. After many cups of coffee, she slipped in beside Therese, and cuddled up to her. She slept fitfully until Caomhán announced the new day shortly after cock-crow.

"Will you stay around while John's here?" Bridie pleaded.

"It's a private matter between the two of you. He wouldn't thank me for butting in on your business."

"Well, I'd thank you. At least let him see the car is there so he'll think you're in your room or something."

"He's hardly going to try anything on here."

"I'm taking no chances."

"I'll go for a walk, but I'll be within shouting distance. If he has any sense at all, I have no doubt but he'll be like an angel out of Heaven today. He surely realises that he can forget about coming again if he tries anything on."

Exactly on the stroke of three a car pulled up outside and John got out. He ran up the front steps, a big bunch of flowers in his hand. From her vantage point behind the lace curtain, Bridie thought that he'd got thin since their time together in London. It made him look athletic. You wouldn't know what he looked like from the way he was dressed on St Stephen's Day.

He tried to give her a peck of a kiss when she opened the door but Bridie turned quickly away. He handed the flowers to Caomhán. The child scattered them on the floor and Bridie left them where they lay, all over the hall. "I'll leave Caomhán with you in the sitting-room," she said, "so that you'll get to know each other."

"It'd be better if you were here. He won't have a clue who I am. As far as he's concerned I'm a stranger."

"This is your Daddy," Bridie said.

"*Daidí na Nollag*?" The only Daddy that meant anything to Caomhán was the Irish name for Santa Claus. That or "*Daideo*"

"Show John what *Daidí na Nollag* brought you." Bridie thought it better not to confuse him any more than was necessary. John was good with children, and soon his son was as much at ease with him as if he had known him all his life. John wound up the young fellow's toy and sang along with the song "*This old man...*" Caomhán was fascinated, and tried to imitate the tune.

Bridie went to the kitchen to get tea, and when she came back Caomhán was sitting on his father's knee, waving his clock, showing her how to get music from it. He jumped up and down, laughing and clapping his hands when the clock played the last line, "This old man comes rolling home." A lump came to Bridie's throat when she saw father and son so alike, so much at ease together.

Therese had been right. John was like an angel. He put no pressure on her, avoided references to the past, talked of nothing but Caomhán and how well she'd reared him. He said that he wanted to stay at home. He hoped they would see each other often. The couple of hours passed so quickly and, after the first nervous moments, so pleasantly that it came as a surprise when they heard Therese's key opening the front door. Was it five o'clock already?

For a moment Bridie thought of asking John to stay for dinner, but something inside her counselled caution. Anyway, his friend's car arrived outside to collect him. They arranged for him to come back again the following Sunday at three.

"If that suits you." He couldn't have been more agreeable.

"I can see now what you saw in him," Therese said, as she studied him from behind the curtain when he was getting into the car. "He's a right film star."

"You can have him, if he's that nice."

"I wouldn't have him as a present, or any man."

"It wasn't as bad as I expected." Bridie was relieved.

"It'll work out all right in time. Isn't there many a separated couple that arrange access to the kids in a civilised way?"

"I suppose you're right."

"Am I ever wrong?" Therese joked.

"You're right an odd time."

"I can see him winning you back."

"Winning! You'd think I was some sort of a prize."

"To him you are."

"I'll try to be civil, for Caomhán's sake. They got on really well and it's no weight on anyone to know their own father."

"I wouldn't agree," Therese said, "but that's another story. It wouldn't surprise me at all to see you back together."

"Are you out of your mind?"

"I don't mind what you decide to do."

"Don't you, Therese?"

"He *is* your husband."

"He was. In law, I suppose he still is."

"That counts for a lot."

"I don't think that I'd have much problem getting an annulment. I was young. I was pregnant. He was violent. I doubt if either of us was mature enough to know what we were going into."

"Why don't you apply for one?"

"I don't want to marry again."

"It would be a way of showing John that you don't want him back."

"In another way it'd be like declaring that Caomhán was illegitimate. I don't want the other kids at school to be calling him a bastard."

"Things like that don't mean anything in this day and age."

"They don't, unless you're the one being called the names. Anyway, they say that you have to answer a lot of questions if you apply for an annulment. It's a kind of a court with priests, asking you about intimate details of your private life, old stagers of priests who know nothing of women or of love."

"How do you know? Some of them dip their wicks now and again."

"Apart from those. I know that there are some very understanding priests but the authorities are hardly likely to put them in charge of marriage courts. They'd be giving annulments as quickly as the others would be marrying."

"That sounds like a little bit of an exaggeration,"

Therese interrupted her in full flow.

Bridie wasn't convinced. "They'd need to give out a lot more of them, because marriage generally seems to be up shit-creek, with or without divorce available. There's an awful lot of children being reared now by just one parent, mostly the mother, of course."

"It does mean a lot to you to be married," Therese commented, "despite what you say about marriage."

"Haven't I got it both ways, married and separated." Bridie shrugged. She decided to keep things at a superficial level.

"If you meet another man?"

"I don't want to meet any man."

"You're young. You're bound to meet someone. It might be harder to get an annulment in a few years."

"I'll take it one day at a time. Anything could happen in a few years. The end of the world might come before that. A man'd want to be a born saint before I'd show any interest in him. And I'd live with him for at least a year before marrying. It wouldn't make any difference to me if I was married or not so long as the relationship was good."

"That's because you're married already."

Bridie winked. "Isn't it to you I am married now, anyway?" She didn't feel like having a deep conversation.

"You are, if you are," Therese laughed.

"There are days when everything looks dark," Bridie said. "On a day like today I couldn't give a damn about anything, least of all about men and marriage, and what might or might not happen."

"They say that men never discuss their feelings," Therese said, "that they're so logical that they never discuss things like we discuss."

"I don't think anything matters to them except the little jewels they have between their legs, big jewels in their own minds, of course."

"Bridie, you shock me," Therese feigned surprise.

"Far too much we talk, I suppose. What does it matter?" Bridie felt giddy. "What about going out for another few scoops?"

"Aren't we overdoing the drink already?"

"It's Christmas. It comes but once a year."

"There's a full cabinet of drink there."

"It's not the drink. It'd be nice to be out with the crowd. You're always saying that I don't go out enough."

Therese would have preferred to stay at home but she didn't want to let Bridie out alone, especially now that John was at home. As soon as she walked into the pub her reluctance fell away. She was among the people, a butterfly in the light, warmly greeted, hugged, even kissed by some of the men on her Board's payroll.

She began to move around, talking, shaking hands, a politician on her rounds, greeting people home for the festival, suggesting they should think about staying, always on the look-out for experienced workers. She was a strong believer in cashing in on the skills people had picked up when they were forced to emigrate.

"Well, and don't tell me little Bridie was let out at last." Peadar Halloran sounded as if he'd been drinking all day. "Is it remission for good behaviour, or what?" He sat down beside Caomhán.

"Daddy," Caomhán said, thinking it was a new word for a man.

"A pity I'm not," Peadar said, "but I might be if I play my cards right. What's wrong with me? Why doesn't your mother come out for a meal with me some time? It's not her I want to eat, but the food."

"Can't you see why?" Bridie indicated her son with a wave of her hand. "I don't have anyone to mind him. Baby-sitters cost a bomb, when you can get them. That's why I had to bring him out tonight. I'll go out for a meal with you all right if you're willing to change his nappy in the middle of the dinner."

"Not the most appetising of prospects between the starter and the main course. Not my idea of an inter-course, if you get my meaning." Peadar laughed at his own joke.

"You're coarse," Bridie told him.

"Not suitable for polite company, am I?"

"You're not the worst," she said lightly. Peadar sat looking at Caomhán for a while with a fixed stare, as if he was trying to solve a difficult problem. "He's as drunk as a skunk," Bridie thought. Eventually he spoke, his voice slightly slurred:

"Couldn't old Thatch-head mind him the odd time?"

"She's at a meeting nearly every night." Bridie had decided that if he was like this she certainly wouldn't be going out with him. She'd enough of drunken men to do her for a long time. She went on, "I never know for sure when she'll be at home. Most of the time she doesn't know herself what kind of a meeting is going to crop up from day to day."

"Meetings," he laughed, raising his glass, "meeting with this."

"That's not true. It's part of her job to be out among people."

"Between me and you," he put his mouth near her ear as if he was going to whisper, but instead said quite loudly, "she's a raging alcoholic." Bridie could feel little drops of spittle hit the side of her face.

"If she was, she wouldn't be so good at her job."

"Is she that good? Or is it all a load of old crap? A lot of slick publicity? A good PR job." Suddenly he sounded sober and articulate again. "I can tell you that most of the politicians haven't much time for her. And neither do I. She put the kibosh on my idea for a small industry."

"I didn't know that."

"This project has not been properly researched, or costed." He quoted from the letter of rejection, putting on a snooty woman's accent, as if it was a personal rejection from Thatch herself.

"Did Therese say that to you?"

"Wasn't her name on the letter?"

"I'm sure she doesn't have time to go into the details of every application. There are at least a hundred and fifty people working in the organisation and that's just in the administration side of things."

"I'm just not good enough for that crowd," Peadar said, scathingly. "I'm bog-Irish. I'm not a foreigner. If I was from Japan or Germany, they'd be licking my arse before and after meals." His voice was faltering again, arse coming out as "arsh".

"I'm sure that you'll be successful if you do some more research on the project." Bridie tried to encourage him.

"What difference does it make?" he spoke very loudly. "I'm not good enough for the old bitch. I'm just another bloody statistic, another failure. I'm not good enough for you either. I'm no good for anything. Full stop."

"You'll feel better tomorrow," Bridie said. "You seem to have a few too many on board at the moment."

"So what? Isn't it Christmas?"

"Too much drink can change your personality," Bridie said, kindly. "This isn't the Peadar I used to know."

"And is it lemonade you're having yourself?" He tasted Bridie's drink. "Make sure that it doesn't change your personality. Or you might start to go out to dinner with the wrong kind of a bloke."

"I know when to stop."

"You know how to stop me anyway, Bridie, to stop me in my tracks." He looked at the bar. "I see your ex up near the counter, big bad John. I wouldn't like to tangle with that fellow now, so I'd better mind my manners. Keep my nose clean, or I could be in trouble there. Or maybe it's only women he beats up."

Because she had her back to the bar, Bridie hadn't seen John. She looked around. He smiled and raised his glass, partly in greeting, partly to show that he was having a soft drink. She turned back to Peadar. "Anything that has happened over the years between me and my husband is none of your business. He's a better man than you ever were, and he's off the drink."

"You're going back to him?"

"I don't want to have anything to do with any man."

"You don't need to when you have that old Thatch-head."

"What are you trying to say?" Bridie looked at him sharply.

"She looks more like a man than a woman, a titless ould cunt, a dry ould ride if I ever saw one." Specks of froth were beginning to form on his lips.

"I don't have to listen to this. Come on, Caomhán." Bridie picked him up and carried him over to where Therese was talking to one of the engineers. "Could you leave me home, please?"

"Sure we've only got here. Make up your mind, Bridie. It was you that wanted to come out in the first place."

"I want to get away from your man. He's hassling me." Peadar was coming towards them. "This project isn't properly researched, or costed," he said sarcastically to Therese, obsessed by his letter of rejection. "You could do with a bit of researching yourself, you dry shite of a yellow-haired ould bitch."

"Is this fellow annoying you?" With the type of hip-charge he used on the football pitch John flattened Peadar on the floor. He held up his hands innocently, as if to say "I never touched him," another trick he'd learned on the field of play. The barman was out in a flash, helping Peadar to his feet, offering him a lift home, smoothing things down, guilty that Peadar had been served so much drink, "too much of the Christmas spirit." After mouthing a few insults and curses at John, Peadar left.

Both Therese and Bridie thanked John. He gave Caomhán a kiss before the women left for home without finishing their drinks. "That's enough of pubs to do us for a while," Therese said when they got back to the house. Later, when it was nearly bedtime, she remarked, "I can't wait to get back to work."

"Thanks very much. You must be awful fed up with us."

"It's not that, and you know it. I wasn't built to be idle."

"We'll miss you from the house, Caomhán and myself." Bridie got in to bed beside her, remarking, "I could see tonight what makes you tick. You come alive when you're out among people. You'd think it was a drug you'd taken when you walked into the crowd."

"It sends the adrenaline through me all right. I love it, but it tires me out, like an actor after a play. It drains me altogether."

"I always knew you were a bit of an actress," Bridie joked.

"I think it comes from being shy when I was young."

"You? Shy? Pull my other leg."

"I'll pull both of them if you're not careful. But I was. I used to hardly open my mouth to anyone. When I went to London, I had to talk, and talk clearly. Nobody there understood my accent. I still hate going into places that are crowded, but when I do, it's like walking on air. It gives me a buzz."

"Did I tell you Peadar said I didn't need a man because I have you?" Bridie's mind was going back over the night.

"Wasn't he right," Therese said jokingly.

"Where would he get an idea like that?"

"He probably didn't mean anything. He was very drunk."

"There's seldom smoke without fire."

"There often is, when you're trying to light one."

"If wit was shit, you'd be constipated." Bridie quoted a line from her secondary schooldays.

"We haven't done anything like that, and even if we did... What happens in this house is nobody's business but our own." Therese sat up in the bed and looked around. "The doors and the windows are closed, the curtains are pulled. Let them think what they like. Let them mind their own businesses."

"They'd have your guts for garters, that crowd in the Gaeltacht Board, if they ever found out that we slept even once in the same bed."

"Are you going to tell them?"

"Are you daft?"

"Then no one will know. End of story."

"I'd hate to see you in trouble on account of me."

"I'm a big girl now. I can look after myself." Therese hugged Bridie to her. "Fuck the lot of them," she said. "Fuck every begrudger in town."

"Will I go down to my own bed?"

"Do whatever you like."

"It's grand and cosy here."

"Don't worry. I won't jump on you."

"It'd be the last jump you'd jump if you did."

"Would it now?" Therese suddenly tickled Bridie, and just as quickly turned her back and pulled all the bed-clothes on top of herself.

"You'll be the death of me." Bridie dragged at the big quilt. They were still giggling when there was a loud knocking on the front door.

"John!" Bridie stiffened in fear.

"Stay quiet," Therese said. "We'll call the guards if he doesn't go away."

It was then they heard a girl's voice call Bridie's name. It was her sister, Susan. Bridie pulled on a dressing-gown and went to the front door. Her sister threw her arms around her. There were neighbouring men with her. Their father had had a heart attack. He was gone, dead, half an hour ago.

Bridie hardly knew what was happening until they reached the house. Her father was being put into an old coffin. It looked grotty. The paint was scraped and the lining torn. Was this some kind of terrible nightmare? She threw herself on top of him, sobbing and shuddering with grief.

"Let her be," her mother said when the undertaker reached for Bridie's shoulder. "You'll have him at the hospital soon enough."

Bridie stood up after a while. She hugged her mother. Hugged Susan and Johnny. The neighbours stood about shamefacedly, not knowing what to do or say. Her mother explained they'd have to take the body to the hospital for a post-mortem examination. It would be different if he was being treated for a heart condition, or some debilitating disease.

"Why is the squad car outside?"

"For the same reason. They have to make a report, make sure that there hasn't been foul play."

"Jesus Christ," Bridie blurted out, "one of us was hardly going to kill him. We love him, love him so much."

"It's the law." her mother patted her back in an effort to console her. "It has to be done. I suppose there are cases..." Her voice trailed off.

When she had liberally sprinkled her husband's body with holy water the lid was put on the coffin. They followed the neighbouring men as they carried it out of the house. His three children rubbed their hands on the glass sides of the hearse as it moved off, as if they could still somehow claw their father back from the dead.

Bridie thought of the old cliché of it being the end of an era. Her father was old. He had been able to do little enough work for ten years now. He'd had a good innings, as people would say. But who could believe that he would no longer sit at the hearth, pipe-smoke and witty remarks coming from the sides of his mouth? He might have belonged to another age. He might have been old-fashioned, narrow-minded maybe sometimes, but he was a lovely man to have had as a father.

When she tried to think back over it later, Bridie felt that the rest of the night ran together. Neighbours visited, porter, cigarettes, tea-making, talk; the priest came at midnight to say the Rosary. Her mother repeated the story of his death to each new person who came into the kitchen, the last things he'd done and said, what he had eaten for his dinner, how he'd seemed so contented as he smoked his last pipe.

Bridie was amazed to find herself laughing from time to time at some famous remark or other attributed to her father, the stuff of local legend. How could she laugh, she asked herself, and Dad lying on a cold marble slab in the mortuary? She thought of his right hand, so crippled with rheumatism that he'd difficulty holding his pipe. Wouldn't he soon be under the ground, clay and worms. She'd cry bitter tears then, but there would be more tea to make, to hand around. She'd find herself laughing. She'd forget that Dad was gone, that his kindly eyes would never sparkle again.

Therese used all her organising skills to help with the arrangements, to inform relatives in the Gaeltacht ghettos of Boston and Huddersfield, to send the funeral times to the local and national papers as well as to the local radio stations. She took care of Caomhán at the same time. She told Bridie not to worry about him until everything was over. However good Therese was to her, Bridie had a nagging feeling at the back of her mind that her father's death was some kind of heavenly revenge for being half happy over Christmas. It was silly, she felt, but it was a real feeling. It was there.

John came to the wake. He sat for a long time with his mother-in-law's hands held in his, listening to her tell every detail of the death. He offered to mind Caomhán until after the funeral. Bridie was very grateful, she told him, but it was better to leave Caomhán in the house he was used to when she herself wasn't with him. "It must be my first night ever away from Caomhán," she thought.

Even when she was in hospital in London his little carry-cot had always been by her side. It felt now as if he was beginning to grow away from her, as if all she loved were slipping away together. She worried about her son until she reminded herself that Therese would be quick to ring if anything was wrong. There was a phone in nearly every house in the country now.

They told her to get some sleep later that night. Otherwise she would be murdered tired the next day, she was told. There would be shopping to be done, the removal to the church, a hundred and one things to be arranged. "How can I sleep and poor Dad gone?" she asked. But sleep she did, her last waking thought being, "Could this really be the same night I climbed into bed beside Therese without a worry in the world on me?" It seemed like ages ago.

Bridie felt very comfortable in her own bed when she woke up some hours later. It was as if she was a little girl again. It was then she remembered why she was there. Dad was dead. The worst was still in front of them, going to the mortuary, seeing him in the coffin, the coffin being closed, the awful hole in the cemetery, the clay rattling on the coffin. But other people went through it day after day. They lived through it, even after a young person died. A day came that they could laugh and joke again as if nothing had happened. But she'd never forget her father.

A memory came to her from away back. He was

minding her while her mother had gone in to Galway. "I mustn't have been much older than Caomhán is now," she thought. She'd cut the thumb of her right hand on a piece of broken glass. She could still see the blood shooting in a spray into the air. Her father got a big black cobweb from the roof of the barn. He wrapped the wound, her hand, the lot in it. He sat with her on his knee until the blood congealed, the bleeding stopped, saved her life probably.

She'd never understood what people meant when they said that the Irish wake was a great consolation to the bereaved. Bridie understood that now that death had come to her own door. It helped people through the hardest times. There was support and comfort in just knowing that neighbours were with you, that there was *comhbhrón* as the Irish language put it, grieving together.

It helped too to have something to do. Therese took Bridie and Susan and Johnny to the city, where they bought clothes for the occasion, for themselves, and for their mother as well. They bought flowers to put on the coffin. By the time they had something to eat before going back to the house it was well into the evening. They began to get ready to go to the hospital.

The old man had been laid out beautifully in his home-spun trousers and waistcoat type "veist," as it was called. He seemed to have a quizzical smile on his lips as if he was mocking death itself. They kissed his cold lips. That was the hardest part, looking on a face you loved for the last time.

The second night wasn't as hard as the first. A large crowd came back to the house from the church, but people didn't wait long. They knew that the family needed sleep. Bridie's mother insisted that she go home that night with Caomhán and Therese, and it was with her friend's arm around her that Bridie slept, a better sleep than she'd have dared to hope for.

The Mass was well planned, thoughtful, consoling. Susan and Johnny read the lessons. Bridie admired their courage. She knew that she couldn't have faced a crowd and read without breaking down. But they had plenty of practice of that kind of thing at school. She and her mother brought the offertory gifts to the altar. Caomhán held tightly to her skirt and carried his grandfather's pipe.

The old priest, Father Jordan, spoke well. He had the reputation of being quick-tempered and surly much of the time but he was kind and thoughtful in times of grief. He'd suffered a lot himself. Two of his brothers drowned as they fished with him from a currach in their youth. Sometimes people thought that he'd never forgiven himself for not dying with them. When he spoke of grief and loss people knew that he knew what he was talking about. Despite his bad manners and temper, they felt his heart was in the right place.

The burial was almost over before they knew it, such was the crush of people coming to sympathise. Some things remained in Bridie's mind: the four members of the family on their knees around the coffin as the priest blessed the grave. The coffin being let down on ropes. The priest throwing clay on the coffin, "Dust thou art..." But the priest was right. She was sure of it. They would see him again. It was easy to imagine him with his pipe in his mouth on the right hand of God. "I hope he doesn't spit too much on the shiny floors of Heaven," she thought, a smile coming to her lips.

A strong hand was laid on her shoulder. John stood by her side, standing with his wife and son in their grief. She appreciated that. He didn't say anything. He didn't need to. Only for the crowd standing about she would have turned into his strong arms at that moment, let him hold her, hug her. Had she been too hard on him? Had he changed, learned his lesson as he said? Should she give him another chance? Should she be with her husband and son instead of getting more and more tangled into Therese's life?

When she realised that it was all over and the people had scatteried, Bridie suddenly burst out crying. Susan had her head on her mother's shoulder, sobbing quietly. Johnny stood on his own, trying to be a man. His reddened eyes betrayed the fact that he too had cried enough. Tears stop eventually when the well empties, she thought, but nothing brings back the one that's gone.

They moved slowly towards the gate, thanking the people that came over to sympathise and say, "I'm sorry for your trouble." Up to now she had thought that clichéd formula to be little more than a meaningless mantra. Now she knew that a seemingly insincere throwaway line meant an awful lot at such a time.

Back in the house again there were more sandwiches to be prepared, the same stories told and retold, the smell of stale tobacco smoke and porter all around the house, Dad's chair empty. Then, as if the tide had gone out, everyone was gone. Bridie offered to stay a few days, but her mother said it was better for herself to face up to reality sooner rather than later. She'd get on with her work in the house and on the land. She had no intention of sitting moping on the hearth.

During the wake and funeral Bridie had felt nothing would ever be the same again. She felt that life should come to a halt because her father was dead. She knew that this was completely irrational, but she was still amazed that life went on as if nothing had happened. People went about their business, talked and laughed, shopped and prayed, collected their pensions on Friday. The sun shone despite her heavy heart. It was as if her father had slipped away unknown to the world.

At first very little time passed without her thinking of him. That gradually changed. She'd notice now and again that hours, even half a day would pass and she wouldn't even have thought of him. Then Caomhán would say "Daideo," and a lump would come to her throat. In all the bittersweet sadness it was lovely to remember him as he was, to find that most of her memories of her father were happy.

By the end of the week she was looking forward to three o' clock on Sunday, when John was to come again. She didn't like the fact that she felt like that. She couldn't say it to Therese, but she was afraid that she was falling in love with him again. She knew now that her feelings for him were a lot stronger than she'd admitted to herself for a very long time.

Bridie felt torn between John and Therese. While she thought of going back to her husband it was hard to imagine life without Thatch. She felt guilty just for sleeping in the same bed as her friend, but what was it most of the time but company and comfort? Or was it? "When all this is over..." she told herself, but she wondered. She was confused and upset as she grieved.

Caomhán recognised his father this time. He ran towards John, and leapt up, as well as he could, into his arms. John hugged and kissed him. Then he threw him up in the air, catching him in his strong hands as he fell free. "Again," Caomhán would say, gurgling with laughter, "again John Daddy."

"Did you hear that I got a job?" was the first thing John said to Bridie. He looked so handsome, smiling from ear to ear.

"Great. What job? What kind of a job?" She felt excited for him.

"In that new woodwork place they're opening just past Furbo. I had an interview and aptitude tests on Friday. They mustn't think that I'm too thick. I'm ready to start in the morning."

"You're definitely staying at home so?" Bridie didn't know whether she felt pleased or apprehensive—a mixture of both, maybe. A job would be bound to do him good, give him security, but did she really want him around? "Your mother will like that," she smiled at him. "I'm sure she likes to have you around."

"I thought that you might like it too."

"I'm glad you got the job. I know it's something you'll enjoy, working with your hands. And Caomhán will be getting to know his father."

"John Daddy." Caomhán pointed a finger at his father. When he saw them laugh, he repeated it, "John Daddy."

"Would you come for a walk with us?" John asked Bridie.

"It might be good for you to have a while with him on your own."

"I don't think he knows me well enough yet."

"After the welcome he had for you just now? Why not? Wait a minute until I get my coat, and wrap him up a bit better."

They walked slowly out the bog road, each parent holding one of Caomhán's hands. He lifted his feet from the road from time to time, swinging between them, allowing himself to be carried along.

"You miss your father?" John broke the silence.

"A lot. It's like having lost part of myself."

"I was like that too after my old man died. Everywhere you'd look you'd expect to see him. I still dream about him as if he was alive."

"I never heard you mention your father before."

"Didn't I?"

"I never remember us having serious conversations."

John didn't like to remember their past. He'd prefer to let sleeping dogs lie. "Have we to go back over all that again?"

"They say that it's good to look back, to learn from past mistakes."

"Well, I've certainly changed. I've learned a lot."

"Me too, too much, maybe." They walked in silence. Bridie kicked a pebble along in front of her. "Do you still think of your father?" she asked after a while, uncomfortable with the quietness.

"Not as often as when he died first. He was dead before I was old enough to get to know him properly, to get to know him right at all, really." He left it at that. Better not mention drink, he thought. She might think it's hereditary.

"When I see Dad's pipe or something..." She was afraid her voice would break.

"I was the same. Cutting grass with a scythe my father was when he dropped dead. I couldn't look at that scythe for a long time without wondering what he was thinking of in his last moments. Was he happy or fed up? Did he know he was near the end, or had he no clue at all?"

"Both of them died suddenly, Caomhán's two granddads."

"That's life. Here today, gone tomorrow." They walked on. Caomhán kicked at a little stone on the road.

"Stop that," his mother said. "You'll ruin your shoes."

"It's imitating you he is," John laughed.

"What do you mean, imitating me?"

"You were kicking a stone yourself a while ago."

"I paid a lot for those shoes for him," Bridie said angrily. "I don't want to see them ruined. Buy him football boots if you want to have him kicking stones."

"All I said was that you were doing the same thing."

"I hope he never imitates some of the things you did."

"It's very easy to vex you these days, Bridie."

"Who's talking? I never hit anyone no matter how angry I got."

"I'm getting tired of this crack," John said. "You really know how to get up my hole. I'll take him out on my own the next time."

"If you get permission."

"Who'll stop me? I *am* his father."

"A fine father. Where were you since he was born?"

"You know well where I was. I was in jail because you informed on me."

"I didn't tell anybody. I wasn't able. I'd just been thrown down the stairs. I suppose you don't remember anything about that. And what did you do then? You left me for dead and went back to bed."

"Fuck this for a crack. A man goes to see his son and all he gets is ould shit." He walked away from them. Bridie turned in the opposite direction, but Caomhán wouldn't go with her. "John Daddy," he said, pointing after his father, dragging at Bridie's hand as he tried to follow him. His mother picked him up and tried to run. Caomhán wriggled and kicked in her arms, shouting, "John Daddy! John Daddy!"

Bridie let him down on his feet on the road and gave him a slap on the backside. His shouts turned to screeches, plaintive cries that went to her heart because she'd never hit him before. She went down on her knees on the road beside him, distraught. She hugged him until he quietened.

They were still in this position when John came back. He was full of regret and apology. Bridie stood up and they walked back towards the house. She listened without answering as he told her how sorry he was, that he would never say another cross word to her, that all he wanted in life was to be able to see his son now and again. She could feel the salt tears on her lips as she walked in silence, wishing life was different, wishing she was dead. Back at the gate of the house she told him she was sorry for bringing up the past. "I've been very upset since Dad died."

"The fault is all mine," he said.

"It was me really."

"I know well that I was responsible. I should never have said anything about the bloody stone." Bridie's tears turned to laughter in a moment. "It's funny that the two of us should be arguing about whose fault it is. There was a time that neither of us would give in about anything."

"It's nice to see you laugh again."

"I cry more often than laugh these days."

"So can I come again?"

"Caomhán couldn't do without you now."

"Next Sunday so." He bent and kissed Caomhán on the forehead.

"At the same time. Good luck with the work tomorrow."

Back in the house Therese asked, "And how is handsome today?"

"I know now that I'll never go back to him anyway," Bridie replied, before telling what had happened. "We're just not compatible. We'd fight like cats and dogs. The smallest thing would set us off, as it did today, and the past would be there like a black cloud hanging over us."

"Well, you're clear in your mind about that much."

"I suppose I still love him in a way," Bridie said, thinking aloud, "but what good is love like that if people can't get along? I've had enough of that kind of love, if you can call it love. It's fine on the stage or the screen but it murders the ordinary woman. Did you ever see the film *Who's Afraid of Virginia Woolf?*"

"I didn't see the film, but I saw the play in the West End. I think I know what you mean: passion isn't always love."

"Why can the two of us get along fine most of the time when John and myself can't? And it's women who are supposed to be the bitches, always fighting and tearing at one another."

"We might just happen to be more compatible. Maybe we understand what the other has been through. Sometimes I think that our kind of sisterhood is stronger than the love of women for men or *vice versa*."

"That's what you call it, sisterhood?"

"Codding me you are now, but sisterhood is a strong part of the bond between us. I think that it's stronger than that though. I know that I love you."

"Don't be going on with silly talk like that."

"Why shouldn't I, since it's true?"

"I'm mixed up enough without having to listen to that kind of *seafóid*. You'd think that it's in competition with John you are."

"I am too, but don't let that stop you from going back to him if that's what you want. I'm not going to put a halter on you."

"I know that I won't be going back to him, not after today. But I think I don't hate him as much as I did. And I'm glad that Caomhán will know his daddy." The little fellow looked up when he heard his name being mentioned. "Poor little mite," Bridie said, "torn between the lot of us."

"Isn't it lucky for him, that he has three parents to love him and look after him."

"There are times I long for the simple life," Bridie said, "times I'm sorry that I didn't have an abortion, didn't get married."

"Didn't meet me?"

"Didn't have any complications in my life."

"You'll be dead long enough," Therese commented. "The reality is now, so count your blessings, a beautiful son..."

"A fucked-up marriage. A job as a servant girl," Bridie sobbed, "and Dad is dead." Therese put her arms around her and they lay fully clothed on the bed, joined, of course by Caomhán and his teddy bear. After a while Therese got a blanket, and covered mother and child as they slept. She began to make plans for going back to work in the morning.

Work was like a drug and she was dying to get back to it. She had enjoyed her Christmas holiday for the most part, in spite of Bridie's father's death. She thought a good holiday was something that relaxed you but at the same time hyped you up with enthusiasm for your work. That was how she felt now. She got a notebook and began to scribble down reminders of what her priorities would be when she got back to her desk. For a moment she was seized with an almost uncontrollable desire to ring her second in command. "Patience," she counselled herself, "he's still on his holidays."

Hours later, after getting to sleep early in order to be well rested for work, Therese was awoken by the telephone ringing.

"Hello," she said sleepily. She thought this might be someone in distress; all she could hear was a kind of hoarse breathing.

"Is there something wrong?" she asked. "Take a few deep breaths and try to tell me what you want to say." It was only then that she began to realise that whoever it was was breathing deeply already, not in distress but with malice. It was a crank caller. A cold sweat began to break out on her back.

"Who's there?" she demanded. The breathing got louder, a kind of a groan with sexual overtones.

"Get off the phone!" she shouted. "I'm calling the guards!"

"Dirty ould cunt," the caller said, and hung up. Therese immediately rang the local Garda station. It was obvious that she'd woken the sergeant; he seemed disoriented and reluctant to get out of bed. She knew she sounded excitable and panicky but she felt there was no excuse at all for his lethargy. "Would you ever get a move on, Tom. We could be in danger here."

"Calm down now like a good girl. There's little enough we can do at this point in time," he said. "We could take a dander down around the phone kiosk in the village all right. There could be some smart alecs going home from the pub with a few too many in them, thinking this is the way to have fun. We caught a few little whippersnappers at that crack a couple of years ago."

"This was no smart alec. It was very deliberate. But you're right. It might be from the kiosk. I heard money going in."

"I suppose I'd better investigate that so."

"Would you ever do it now, Tom, or he'll be miles away before anyone has a chance of catching up with him."

"Don't get your hopes up, Thatch, um, Therese. Come to think of it, it may not have been from that kiosk that the call was made at all." A very kind man, the sergeant had a reputation for being more interested in talk than in action. Therese couldn't believe that an officer of the law could be so slow. "Would you ever get a move on now, Tom," she said, "and you might catch him. Please"

"The Mounties always get their man," he said. "Patience is the key to good police work. Patience and planning. Don't worry your pretty head about it. I'll send for the squad from Oughterard."

His patronising tone made Therese cringe but she decided there was no point in taking issue with him. It would only cause further delay. "We could be dead in our beds before that comes."

"I can tell you now that you're in absolutely no danger. There have been many studies done about this type of behaviour. And I'm not talking about this country. I'm talking world-wide."

"If I rang the superintendent, would he hurry up

the squad car?" Therese tried to shake him out of his laziness.

"I can tell you now that it would be a very expensive call. The super is gone to a police conference at the other side of the world. Serious business, and not some kind of a junket as you might be inclined to think. In Australia, to be exact. Down under, as they say themselves. He won't be back until the far end of the month."

"Well, who *is* in charge?" Therese said angrily. "We might all be down under before long, down under the ground, if you don't do something."

"I'm in complete control, Therese, dear, and if you have a minute's patience I'll get a biro and a notebook." He put on his official voice when he took up the phone again. "At what time precisely was the offending telephone call made?"

He went on to ask had anyone been sacked recently from work who might have a gripe or grievance against her. She couldn't think of anyone. He advised her to hang up the moment the offending caller rang again, to ring the barracks immediately. "Of course," he reminded himself, "that'll be no good, because I will be out searching for the culprit."

"By the way, what kind of person makes calls like this? Are they usually dangerous?" Therese immediately regretted having asked the question, as the reply would only cause further delay.

"They're usually lonely. After a few drinks the frustration breaks out in ways like this. Often they think they're in love with the person they're calling. They want to hear their voice. And more often than not, of course, as in this case, that person is away out of their reach."

"If you love someone you're hardly likely to call her a dirty cunt."

"Well, that's part of the frustration too. I read a report..." Therese cut him short:

"You seem very casual about it all, Tom."

"Did you know that my area has the lowest amount of unsolved crime in Ireland? Don't worry one little bit. The Mounties will get their man. If you'll excuse me now, I'll call Oughterard, and order the squad."

Therese laughed as she suddenly realised that it was probably personal courtesy to her as a woman that had delayed the sergeant so long on the phone. Then she began to think of the man with the strange breathing lurking around the house. When the wind rattled something outside she shook Bridie, woke her up, told her what had happened.

Bridie's courage amazed Therese. "Why didn't you call me when it happened?" she asked. She went around the house to make sure that every door and window was secure. Satisfied about that, she brought the heavy iron tongs from the fireplace to the bedroom, bringing the poker for Therese. "If anyone breaks in here, he'll have a fight to get near either of us," she said.

"I never thought a phone call could have me so scared," Therese said. "My knees are literally knocking together."

"I feel brave now, but when I was married to John and he started to get violent my knees used to get weak. I couldn't put up a fight at all, I just stood there and took it. But this is different, we're in it together."

"It's awful to think that a person can be turned into a shivering jelly in a few minutes," Therese said, cuddling close to her friend. "I suppose that's how the

Nazis and the likes of them were so successful. Sheer terror."

"I remember wondering when we were told about it at school," Bridie said, "why the prisoners in the camps didn't swarm all over the guards. They were going to die anyway, and there were a lot more of them than there were guards. But I learned about fear after that, what it can do to you." She caressed Therese's hair as she talked.

"No wonder it's so hard to prove rape. If a woman gives in out of fear they think she's looking for it."

"I could fight anything tonight," Bridie said bravely; "at least I think I can. Tomorrow I might be shivering like a leaf."

"We'll have to get an alarm system," said Therese, who was still white in the face.

"At least we have the phone."

"It's too easy to cut the wires. The worst about these houses is that they're built for the view. There are no neighbours near enough, not like the ribbon development down by the main road."

"What use would an alarm be either, when there's no house nearby?"

"At least the noise might scare someone off. They ring very loudly. Someone would come from someplace."

"I wonder who it was?" Bridie asked.

"I didn't recognise the voice. It was low and husky, but he might just have been putting it on. I suppose a person couldn't do a job like mine without making some enemies. But why should it happen now of all times? It could have to do with my ideas for the television station, anything."

"I doubt if it's business. Love, more likely. Or hate."

"Could it be John?"

"I wouldn't be surprised, if he was drinking, but he's not. Anyway it's me he'd have it in for, not you," Bridie said. "Did you mention him to the sergeant?"

"Not at all. That would really sound like jealousy or revenge or something. Anyway I'd be very surprised if it was him."

"Nothing would surprise me if he was on the piss." Bridie thought for a moment. "I suppose I don't really appreciate the effort he's making for Caomhán's sake. He was very fond of it. I wouldn't have believed he'd manage without it."

"What about your friend that caused the racket in the pub? He called me a few choice names that day."

"Peadar Halloran isn't my friend. Not after that. I'd be surprised if it was. But with drink you never know. The carry-on of him that day surprised me too," Bridie said.

"Fear is bad enough if you can put a name or a face on someone. This is like trying to fight a ghost." Therese was out of bed again pacing the room. "Do you think John really has changed?"

"I think there's a lot of violence in him that he doesn't know how to control. He certainly couldn't when he was on the jar. Would you ever sit down," Bridie said, "all that walking is making me nervous."

"I'd prefer to face the devil himself than some nameless, faceless fucker." Therese sat down on the bed.

"I thought you didn't believe in God or devil."

"I don't believe in them in the daytime, but on a night like this..."

Bridie prepared tea. "We need something stronger than that." Therese got a bottle from the cupboard and poured whiskey into the cups. The cup fell from her hand with fright when the telephone rang again. Bridie picked it up quickly and shouted angrily into it, "Fuck off with you, you dirty bastard."

"I beg your pardon?" It was the sergeant, asking was everything all right. Apprehension changed suddenly to uncontrollable hilarity. The women couldn't stop laughing at the incongruity of it all.

"Are you sure that you're not having me on?" He sounded as if he was quite peeved. "Is there some kind of a party going on there? Is this someone's idea of a joke? Am I being taken for some kind of a ride?"

"I was sure that it was the same fellow that called earlier," Bridie apologised. "I never expected that it could be anyone else at this time of the night. I was so sure..." She didn't know what to say.

"Hello, Tom." Therese took the phone and asked matter-of-factly, "Well, did you find anyone?"

"The squad came a while ago, and we drove around every inch of the place, up and down every by-road and boreen from the beach back up to the bog. There wasn't sight nor light of a sinner to be seen."

"Well, thanks for calling back, Tom. I'll get in an alarm as soon as I can, one that will have a connection with the barracks. If we think of anyone that might be responsible, I'll let you know. I'm sorry for the inconvenience, but it's a very frightening situation for a woman, or a couple of women, to be in."

"I understand that very well."

"Thanks very much, Tom." She didn't leave him time to start another spiel. "Goodnight, or should I be saying 'good morning' at this stage?" She hung up.

"You can be so sweet at the fancy talk." Bridie was laughing at her when she got off the phone. She put on a mock imitation of Therese's accent. "Yes, Tom, no, Tom, kiss me arse, Tom."

"Tom isn't the worst. He's a lovely man in fact, but he's not the most efficient policeman in the world. He's too nice for that kind of a job."

They slept fitfully for the rest of the night. When Therese woke up around six the electricity was out, there was lightning and a great thunder shower. Hailstones beat on the window. That scared her. She shook Bridie awake, and asked her to put her arms around her. She was almost asleep again when she sat up with a start.

"There's someone in the room."

Bridie listened. She heard a light footfall. She reached down beside the bed for the tongs: "Who's there?" she asked, fear like a cold hand on her back.

"Mammy." Caomhán had climbed out of his cot, wakened by the thunder. Despite the absence of the usual nightlight, he'd made his way to their bedroom. Bridie pulled him in between them and he fell asleep almost immediately, soothed by the warmth of their bodies. Therese and Bridie talked until dawn crept in behind the curtains.

❦

John's eyes were stuck together when he woke up on Monday morning. His head felt as if there was a sledge breaking stones inside it. His mouth was dry and there was a terrible taste on his tongue. He thought that he was still in prison until he heard his mother moving around the kitchen. He was in his own bed in his own room, at home. He saw the bottle beside the bed, a couple of inches of poteen at the bottom of it. "Oh,

Christ," he thought. He'd gone on the tear the previous day.

"I have the flu, Mam," he answered when his mother knocked at the door and asked was he getting up. "I have a sore throat. I'm hoarse. You can hear it in my voice." He fell asleep again, dreaming he was in the prison yard. He was playing football, beating the Cockneys at their own game. He dribbled past two of them and slammed the ball against the bottom of the high wall on which a rectangle of paint represented the goal posts. It was after one o'clock when he woke up again. The smell of poteen was the first thing he noticed.

He tried to remember what exactly had happened after he'd left Bridie and Caomhán the day before. Things came back gradually. Micil, the lad who'd collected him from the house, had brought him back through Connemara for a spin. It was like old times, going from pub to pub, having the crack with the lads, who looked on him as some kind of a hero because he was such a good footballer.

His time in jail was ignored and might yet become legend as some kind of political offence, he thought. He was that kind of a bloke, lucky. He remembered having a pint of Cidona in the pub in Rossaveal, even though a lot of pressure was put on him to have what the lads called a "real drink."

Further west they had visited a house in which Micil had an eye on one of the girls. The man of the house had brought out the poteen. "The best cure of all for the cold," he'd winked. Although John had said that he was on the dry, a hot poteen punch was put into his hand. The best of stuff, the man said, "*tús an phota.*" He had thought one would do no harm. It might even shake off the cold. It was good stuff, softened by the hot water and sugar, easy to drink, too easy.

This was poteen country, where the writ of Gall or Gael never really ran. Sergeant after sergeant came to the area vowing to put an end to it, and ended up frustrated. They tried everything: speedboats, tracker dogs, helicopter overflies. They'd had some success. They broke up barrels, stills, spilled wash, confiscated gas cylinders, won battles, lost the war. Fines and breakages just became part of the business's expenses. "Rebel country," John thought, where neither Church nor state held sway, except in a superficial sort of a way.

The man of the house told of the efforts made to stop it by the Redemptorist missionaries in his own youth, especially *an Misean Mór,* the famous Aranman, *Sagart Twenty.* Hellfire and crucifixes smashed on church floors had been as ineffective as the efforts of peelers and civic guards in their own time. The big missionary claimed he started his own campaign against the demon poteen when he was at a funeral. There weren't four men able to stand up steadily enough to carry the remains. The women had carried the coffin.

Their host acknowledged that poteen could be dangerous. He spoke of men who had died from alcoholic poisoning, others who had died in drains or in the sea because they lost their way as they went home stocious drunk. He put that all down to "bad stuff." Some people used bleach to clear the colour from the drink. Others made it too quickly because of the pressure of the law.

"If the guards would only back off and let people

make it properly," he'd said, "it would be every bit as good as 'parlaimint'." This was the popular name given to shop whiskey in the Gaeltacht. The old man had lifted up his own glass of the clear liquid. "This is the good stuff, the stuff that'll put hair on your chests."

John was amazed he'd such a clear memory of that part of the night but that he was so confused about the rest. He remembered being in one of the hotels in Carraroe at some stage after that, and in another pub not far from the dance-hall. They went in to the dance towards the end of the night, but didn't stay long.

The place was packed to the door with young and old, Joe Dolan on stage, the man from Mullingar as good as he ever was, although one of the lads had said he'd soon be pension age. "He'll soon have the free travel going around to the dances." They'd had a good laugh about that.

They'd sat in the car for a while, drinking the hard stuff from the bottle, girls on their knees, skitting and laughing. He couldn't even remember their names now, something like Felicity and Madeleine. Maybe they'd just made them up. They certainly didn't seem like local names, although the girls could spout Irish to beat the band. They were probably no more than fifteen or sixteen, wild but not willing to go too far. Yet anyhow.

John hadn't touched a woman for so long. He couldn't remember which of the girls it was but she was a gamy bit of stuff, and some kisser. Before long she was swallowing his tongue and darting her own into his mouth in response. He had slipped his hand up under her bra without any complaint. She had lovely soft, firm tits. When he flicked her nipples with his fingers he thought that she was going to get weak. He hadn't lost his touch despite his lack of practice.

She had stopped him though when he tried to open the zip of her jeans. She allowed him to caress her through them instead. He couldn't be sure, but he thought the girl in front was pulling Micil's wire. He thought his own one might get around to doing the same even if she wasn't prepared to go any further. Half a loaf was better than no bread as far as he was concerned. The least a girl might do after getting a man worked up was a blow job, or as a last resort just wank him off.

He'd managed to get her hand to the front of his pants when they heard Joe breaking into *Jailhouse Rock*, and the girls were out of the car like a shot and back into the hall. Micil had followed them, leaving him the bottle. He thought he must have fallen asleep on the back seat of the car. He remembered nothing else until he awoke in his own bed. "Maybe I even had the ride without remembering it," he thought ruefully.

He needed another punch now to clear his head. This would be the very last drink of his whole life, he told himself. He regretted having broken out again on the booze, but it was a once-off. He really did have a cold. Bridie would never need to know. Whatever chance there was of getting herself and Caomhán to come back, the drink would blow it. She was right too. The drink had caused all their problems. But one night after two years... A man deserved that much of a reward. And he was really suffering for it now with the father and mother of a hangover.

He took a swig from the bottle but it tasted terrible. How could he make a hot drop unknown to his mother? "Tea," he thought. He'd make a pot of tea and put the poteen through it in the bedroom. "You're a genius," he told himself. He pulled on his trousers and went up to the kitchen, plugged in the kettle. It seemed to take ages to boil. A watched pot. "At least I have the place to myself for the moment," he thought. "I don't have to face a barrage of questions."

His mother was out. He could see her through the window, giving hay to the cattle. He made strong tea with plenty of sugar before putting some of the poteen through it. He put the bottle with the drop that was left in it up the sleeve of his good jacket, the sleeve resting in the side pocket. He was definitely getting off the jar, but a man couldn't be too careful. You wouldn't know when the flu might strike again.

As cold as it was he opened the room window, and smoked a cigarette at the same time. This would hide the smell of the drink. He pulled the blankets up over his clothes to keep himself warm. The coarseness of the poteen had been masked by the hot sugary tea. He felt much better as the hot liquid circulated through his veins. "I'll be back to myself in no time," he said aloud.

For a second he thought he was in a telephone box, trying to ring Bridie, telling her how much he loved her. The blonde bitch who had answered the phone started giving out to him. A dream? He shook his head and came back to reality. The hard stuff could play funny tricks. He'd often heard it said that it really didn't affect a person until the following day, that even a drink of water could set you off again. Wasn't it just as well he was giving it up for good.

He thought of his mother out after the cattle while he lay in bed. "I'll have to make it up to her." He felt lousy. Something about hurting the ones we love went through his mind. "Well, I'm never going to hurt Mam or Bridie or Caomhán ever, ever again," he promised the picture of Our Lady of Lourdes. "Or you either, or Jesus. I'm turning over a new leaf." He jumped off the bed.

"Oh, holy fuck!" John suddenly remembered that he was supposed to be at work that morning. He searched for the letter he'd got from the firm, found the phone number. He went out to the hall and rang the number.

"Bring your doctor's certificate with you when you come in," the girl said when he had made his excuse. "A virus or something that came on me out of the blue, hot and cold shivers, vomiting and, saving your presence, a dose of the runs."

"But I'm not that sick," he said, when she told him he would definitely need a doctor's certificate. "It's just one of these twenty-four or is it forty-eight hour things, here today and gone tomorrow."

"It's Gaeltacht Board policy that employees reporting absent from work have to provide a doctor's certificate. You might get away with it any other day of the week, but certainly not on the Monday morning after the holidays. The Chief Executive is very strict about that. She had a list before lunch time of all the absentees. Sorry about that," the girl said sympathetically, "but I'm not the one that makes the rules."

"The Chief Executive. That's the blonde they call Thatch?"

"The very one."

"The dirty ould cunt," he said, as he hung up the phone. "It's bye bye to that job." What doctor would give a certificate to a man with a hangover from poteen? John was angry. This blonde bitch was coming before him at every turn. "I'll have to get my wife and son out of that house. The old witch has a bad influence on Bridie, her head full of women's liberation crap. Independence." He said the word as if it was a curse.

He'd heard it said in the bar on Stephen's Day that that Thatch one was a woman's woman. Questions were asked as to why she never let any man get close to her, for all her flirting with them. One of the lads had sworn that he knew someone that knew her in London years before, that she was definitely one of them. "Wouldn't you know by the look of her, the short hair and everything, as butch as they come."

John hadn't believed it. Not with Bridie anyway. Unless that was why Bridie was so distant with him. But a woman like Bridie would have nothing to do with something unnatural like that. Not unless she'd changed a lot from the sexy young filly he'd married. Bridie was no woman's woman, that was for sure. She knew what a man had it for. And it wasn't for stirring his tea.

That girl the night before had reminded him of what he was missing. Why should a man married in the eyes of God and the church have to go looking elsewhere for what his wife was supposed to provide? He'd heard a young priest as much as say one time that it was the ride itself that was the sacrament. Not in so many words maybe, but that was definitely what he'd meant. Hadn't she said, "For better, for worse," as well as he had. He was being denied his God-given rights.

"Put up or shut up," he said aloud to himself. "If she doesn't come back I'll take the child from her. My mother can look after him as good as the next woman."

If the word got around that your one was one of them, there'd be no way his child would be allowed to be reared in that house. What judge would allow the likes of them to make a nancy-boy out of his son? John asked himself.

He told himself that he'd have to show more interest in the land. If he really got down to it he could make a living out of that just as much as he could from carpentry. "They can shove their jobs and their Gaeltacht Board," he said to himself, making it pun with Jailtacht. He liked that. "And I'll say it to that blonde bitch too when I meet her. On second thoughts, better not, not until Bridie is out of that house anyway."

Maybe I could buckle down to the bit of land too, he thought. A bit of drainage would get rid of the rushes. He'd get in more sheep, run some of them on the commonage. He had heard lads in the pub say there were good headage payments, any scrawny old sheep at all qualified. Then he could do a bit of lobster fishing maybe in the summer, sell the odd trailerload of seaweed. "I could pick cockles for the Bretons if it went to that. Sure the world is my oyster." He liked that, "the world my oyster," and him talking about fish. "The old brain cells aren't all gone yet."

Despite his mother's best efforts the land had gone to rack and ruin with weeds and rushes. It needed a man's hand. He remembered the efforts they made when he was a young fellow to cut thistles, clear ragwort and dock. It was the law of the land at the time. You could be prosecuted for having noxious weeds. There were signs up in the post office about it and the sight of a guard on a bike sent men scurrying for scythes and sickles to get rid of the poisonous weed.

Not that the thistle was poisonous. He was very small when his father had told him of the blind man who'd been driven by pony and trap to buy a farm of land. "Tie the horse to a thistle," the blind man had said. "But there aren't any thistles," his driver answered. "Drive on so," was the blind man's instruction. "If it can't grow thistles it can't grow anything." There had been good times with his father too, he thought.

He could see himself now, a teenager with a scythe tackling a field of thistles the way a military general tackled his enemies. He drew up plans, skirmished around the edges, picked off the scouts and outriders one by one, drove a swathe though the middle to split the enemy forces. Then he tore into the remaining thistles with fierce abandon, flaying troops with great sweeps of his scythe until all the mighty had fallen.

John went to the bathroom, shaved and showered, put on clean clothes. That made him feel much better, although he still had a touch of the shakes from the hangover. One hair of the dog, two at most, would settle that. He was ready to go out the door when he met his mother coming in from the farmyard in an old dirty gabardine coat and wellingtons. She looked as if she was in bad form.

"I thought that you were supposed to be at work today?"

"Didn't I tell you," he lied, "the gangerman on the job told me yesterday that they won't be starting for a couple of weeks. The machines haven't come through yet. They're held up by a dockers' strike in Liverpool, it is, I think. Somewhere over across the pond, anyway."

"A lazy excuse," she said. He felt lousy about letting her down. He'd never been any good at telling her lies.

"It's true for me, Mam. I don't know will I bother

waiting for that job. Those strikes drag on and on. I'll get something in the city, or I might even get down to working the land. I was looking at you out in the field a while ago, and I was thinking that the farming is a nice enough number."

"Take a right look at me," she said, pointing at her work clothes. "Is that what you call a nice number?"

"You could take it easy if I was running the place, doll yourself up, help me out the odd day, maybe."

"Farming is a waste of time since that European crowd took over the country."

"A man would have the dole. He might be just as well off."

"Yes, and every morning like this morning, too lazy to get up, especially every Monday morning."

"Ah, Mam, that's not fair."

"Cows don't wait for a hangover to clear. A man would be better off working, with a few cattle on the land, more of a pastime than anything else. They're handy for paying the bigger bills. But I can do that much myself for another couple of years anyway. Long enough I'm doing it. I'd prefer to see you bringing in a weekly wage. It might help to straighten you out."

"I was thinking that if I was at home working the land, Bridie and Caomhán might come to live here, be a real family." He knew of old how to soften up his mother.

"How is Caomháinín?" Her heart melted at the mention of her grandson. "You'll have to bring him here some day. If you can get your wife's permission." She was always good for a dig.

"Of course he can come. Any time that suits you. Sure Bridie and myself are getting on great now."

"Has she any talk of coming back to you?"

"I don't want to put pressure on her at the moment. After the ould fellow's death and everything, she's that bit emotional. She thinks it's great, though, that the young fellow is so fond of me. Do you know what he calls me? John Daddy. Isn't that a good one? He's mad about me altogether. You'd think he knew me all his life. It's true, the old saying: blood is thicker than water."

"Tell her that she won't have to put up with me if she wants to come and live here," his mother said.

"What do you mean?" He was shocked. "You're not thinking of pulling out, surely?"

"I'm not thinking of going into the County Home or anything," she answered, jokingly, "but I could get a mobile, one of them big caravan things, or you could build me one of those little granny flats."

"That's a great idea." John looked at his mother with a new sense of admiration. "You're sure you wouldn't mind? Those mobiles might be cold. I'll build you a nice dry little chalet for what one of them would cost."

"You should never have two women in the same house, in the same kitchen, anyway. We'd fight like cats."

"Tomorrow morning I'll make out a list of the stuff I'd need to build a chalet. There might even be a bit of a grant out of it."

"It couldn't be done that quickly. You'd have to get planning permission, and they're very sticky about that now, especially on the other side of the main road. They don't want to block off the view of the sea from the tourists."

"Typical government," John commented. "Put the

stranger before your own. If it was a German or a Yank they'd have no bother."

"If you were to join the Cumann they might hurry it up for you. Or you could see the Minister, Saturday at the clinic."

"Is he a doctor or something?"

"That's what they call where you can meet the politicians. In the back room of the pub beyond, just like going in to confession."

"I'll look into that. Bridie'll be delighted to hear about it."

"Supposing she doesn't want to come back?"

"If she doesn't, I'm thinking of trying to take Caomhán from her."

"How would you rear a child?"

"I thought that you might help me."

"I was long enough changing nappies."

"Still you wouldn't like to see your own flesh and blood reared by a stranger."

"Aren't most of my grandchildren being reared by strangers in foreign parts? I wouldn't take a child from its mother unless she was a complete bitch altogether. As far as I can see, she's making a great job of rearing him."

"Bridie is fine herself," John frowned, as if he was finding difficulty in telling her, "but I have my doubts about that one that she's working for."

"Thatch? Sure a finer woman never stood in Connemara. Hasn't she put the Gaeltacht Board on its feet."

"I don't like to have my son in the same house as her." He knew there was no one better than his mother to spread a rumour, if he could sow the seed.

"What fault have you with Thatch? Sure you know

nothing at all about her."

"I heard a few things in the pub about her private life I wouldn't like to repeat, and that you wouldn't like to hear."

"I wouldn't take the slightest bit of notice of what people say in pubs," his mother said dismissively. "It's well known that she likes her jar, but she carries it well, and does a good job. What else are they saying about her? That she's fond of the men? What woman isn't? It's a free country, and a lot of things have changed since you went away."

"That's what they're saying, that she *isn't* fond of men."

"You don't mean...? You don't mean that unnatural carry-on between two women, what do they call it?"

"That's what people are saying."

"That's just the crowd trying to get her out of that job. She's too successful, that's her problem. It's all politics, and dirty politics at that. I know that she's not on our side of the fence, but that doesn't mean she's not doing a good job."

"Suppose that it's true?"

"You don't think Bridie...?"

"Why doesn't she want to come back to her husband?"

"If I thought for one minute that my grandson was in a house where there was that kind of carry-on, I'd take him out of it myself."

"I might need help, to get a solicitor, if I find out that it's true."

"You can rely on your mother." She looked more disgusted than angry.

"That's only if she doesn't come home of her own

accord. She might be glad enough to get away from that one if she was sure of a place to go to."

"You should get working on organising that granny flat as soon as you can. If she had a place of her own..."

"You're the best, mother." He gave her a little hug as he passed her on his way to the door. "I hope I'm not smelling of cowshit," he thought, as he headed for the pub.

All he needed was a couple of brandies and ports, he felt. Settle the stomach. He'd go off it then. A couple of pints for a good night's sleep and he'd be as right as rain in the morning. He'd have great news for Bridie on Sunday, their own house. His mother was a real angel.

There was a great welcome for him in the pub when it was seen that he was taking a drink again. There was a good atmosphere. Some of those who'd come home for Christmas hadn't gone back yet. Others were on their way home from work. He saw Thatch sitting near the big open fire in animated conversation with a grey-haired man. He went to the other end of the bar and ordered a brandy and port and a pint. He'd hardly tasted his drink when another pint was placed beside it.

Johnny Fadden, the long-serving secretary of the GAA club, stood beside him, beckoning to the barman to put John's second drink on his slate. He'd heard that John had got a job and that he'd be staying at home. "Congratulations." He shook his hand. If he hadn't a job already, he would have been the first man to get him one, he said. They were going to make a big effort in the Gaeltacht football competition, as well as in the county championships. John's return had been like an answer to prayer.

"We're in the senior grade this year." He elbowed John good-naturedly as he spoke. "The shoulder and the boot are all right in intermediate football, but for senior you need a touch of class." He clapped his new-found recruit on the back. "When it comes to class, there are few classier than yourself." He smiled from ear to ear, porter froth hitting John in the face like little snowdrops. He'd never smelt fouler breath.

"Class and skill." He made great play of punning "class" with the Irish word for a trick, *cleas*. "You have all the tricks in the book, the classiest footballer born and reared west of the Corrib." He qualified his statement, to leave himself out of it, "In this generation, that is."

"I haven't trained in an age," John said, when Johnny asked him would he play on Sunday.

"There's no better training than match practice. You've got the skill, and the man that has skill never loses it. It's like learning to ride a bike." He hit John in the ribs with his elbow. "Or riding anything else. Once you can do it, you never lose it."

"This isn't the best training in the world," John indicated his pint, "but I'm giving it up tomorrow."

"There's no harm in a couple of pints. Do you remember the Connacht final of..." He was away down memory lane, telling John of the best match he'd ever played in his life, long before the younger man was born. "I never told this to anyone else." John had no doubt that he'd heard it six or seven times, the only difference being that the six pints Johnny had drunk before the match had now gone up to eight. There probably wasn't a man in the bar who couldn't repeat Johnny's stories, word for word. "Have I to put up with this for the rest of the night?" he asked himself.

"It would be worth putting up with it," he thought, "for the sake of getting back in the team." That would be one way of keeping out of trouble and keeping himself fit and happy at the same time. Johnny was a selector as well, as nearly everything else and he didn't like to be slighted in the public house. Then John remembered that he was to see Caomhán on Sunday. Weren't there six other days in the week to do that?

He thought that he'd much prefer to visit the house on a weekday, when Thatch was at work. He hated "that one" because he blamed her for the fact that he had no job. And maybe he'd have a chance of Bridie while the other one wasn't there. Not that you could do much in front of the child. Even an old hug would do a man good. "Who knows? She might even go out with me some night. And then..." He leaned against the counter, amused. "If I don't think of something else, I'll end up with a horn on me big enough for all in the bar to see."

Bridie liked football, he remembered. Wasn't it after a match they'd met that very first time when he'd swept her off her feet? He thought of the old Irish phrase "*cac sa tobar.*" Well, he had well and truly shat in his own well, but that was then and this is now. If he played his cards right, who knows? He decided to ring Bridie to see would she mind if he changed the visit from Sunday. He couldn't think of her number offhand. Much as he despised her, he decided to ask Thatch.

He excused himself from Johnny, saying that he had to ring his wife and went to ask Therese the number.

"I thought you knew it already."

"I'd it written down, but I left it in my other jacket."

"The jacket you had on last night?"

"What has last night to do with it?"

"You rang me." She watched his eyes, hoping to find out if he was the culprit, the man who had done the heavy breathing.

"I rang you?" He remembered his earlier flashback, but it was too vague.

"About two o'clock in the morning?"

"Are you saying that I rang you last night?"

"It's me that's asking you."

"Is that why you gave me the sack today?"

"We have our lines crossed here somehow," Thatch said, with apparent nonchalance. "I didn't sack anyone today."

"I was told that you said I wasn't to go in tomorrow if I wasn't in today."

"That does sound like company policy," Thatch said calmly. "You need a doctor's certificate, or a genuine excuse. If someone can provide that, there's no problem. In fact I didn't even know you *were* working. I'm not privy to everything that goes on in the associate companies."

"I was to start today, but something completely unexpected came up. My mother was taken ill."

"I'm sorry to hear that. Is she all right now?"

John was momentarily taken aback by Therese's care for his mother's health. "Some kind of a slack she had, it came on all of a sudden, something to do with diabetes as far as I know." He made it sound as vague as possible, in case Thatch ever met his mother and enquired about her health.

"There has obviously been some kind of a

misunderstanding. The rule we have is to prevent absenteeism due to drinking. It's a way of assuring foreign companies that the Irish reputation for boozing isn't really true." She looked around the bar and lifted up her own glass. "Though you could fool me sometimes," she joked. "That's all right though, outside working hours."

"So when can I start?"

"If the doctor who attended your mother writes a note, I'm sure the company you work for will accept it. It's out of my hands at this stage. Sorry."

"You don't want me to have a job at all," John said aggressively.

"Each company is independent." Therese shrugged her shoulders. "I lay down general rules. They implement them."

"You don't want me to have a job, in case Bridie comes back to me."

"That's complete nonsense. Here, you came to ask me for Bridie's number." Therese wrote it down. "We'll discuss work on Sunday, maybe, if you're sober when you call to see Caomhán. If you genuinely want work, I personally will see that you get it."

"I might stick you to that." He felt like telling her where to stick her job, but he knew that wouldn't go down well with Bridie. He went out to the payphone.

"Did you ring here last night?" she asked as soon as he got through.

"You're the second person to ask me that in the last ten minutes." He told her he'd got the number from Thatch. "It must have been a lousy call that has the two of ye worked up about it."

"The guards are investigating it."

"I care about you, Bridie, you and Caomhán. If I get

the cunt that did it... He'll have me to answer to."

"Have you been drinking?"

"Me?" What was the point in denying it? Thatch had seen him. "I was murdered with an ould cold. My mother gave me a drop of punch. And then the lads came and asked me to play a match on Sunday, so I decided to have a pint with Johnny Fadden. You know what Johnny's like. If you don't have a drink with him you're in the bad books. I'll be playing Sunday." He kept talking, hoping that she'd forget that he had been drinking.

"I thought you were coming to see Caomhán on Sunday."

"Isn't that why I'm ringing, to ask you to change my visiting hours. Jesus, it's beginning to sound like a hospital, with visiting hours and everything."

"What about Saturday so?" Bridie asked him. "You'll be working every other day of the week. It's great about the job. I'm really pleased for you."

He thought it better not to upset her any more by telling her he no longer had the job. Soon enough she'd hear it from that bloody blonde bitch, he thought, but she'd probably have got over it by Saturday. Or maybe he'd have another job by then.

"Saturday so," he said.

"I'm telling you now, for once and for all, John. If you want to see Caomhán on a regular basis, give up the drink now."

"I've just finished my very last drink ever."

"How many times have I heard that?"

"You're too hard on me, Bridie."

"Were you drinking last night?"

"What is this? The Garda station?"

"You promised." He was about to deny it, but what

if she met someone who had seen him in Carraroe? "I had a couple of scoops, a good couple of hot whiskeys if it comes to that. For the cold, mainly."

"It must have come on very quickly," Bridie said. "I didn't hear a sniff out of you when you were here."

"It was coming on for a while, the germs incubating, as they say. Sure they say there's no cure for the common cold, just have a few drinks and wrap up well."

"So what you're really telling me is that you got blotto last night?" John knew from her tone of voice that Bridie was in fairly good form, not too upset about his batter of drink, but cute enough to find out how much he'd had all the same.

"I had a few scoops. It's Christmas. My first Christmas back home for a long time. Will I have to get permission to piss soon?" He remembered school, *"Bhfuil cead agam dul amach?"*

"You don't need any permission from me. Do what you like, but if you want access to Caomhán... I know what drink does to you."

"How many times have I to tell you I'm finished with it?"

"Don't talk. Do." Bridie smiled to herself when she found she was repeating one of Therese's mottoes.

"It's OK if I come to see him on Saturday so?"

"I'll see you then." Bridie wondered if she'd been too hard on him. "I'm glad to see you getting back to the football again. There was no better man." She paused, before adding, "In your day."

"I hope to show you on Sunday that my day isn't done yet." He laughed, and seeing she was in good form, asked, "One more thing. Would you mind if I brought Caomhán to see my mother?"

"Why not? She *is* his grandmother too."

"Would you like to come with us?"

"It'd be better to bring him on his own the first time. She might feel a bit awkward with me around."

"Do you know, you might be right."

"Don't forget what I said about the bottle. I'm very serious about that." She tried to say it as lightly as she could.

"I've given it up already. I won't even drink the pint that's left on the counter. The only one of this family that will have a bottle from now on is Caomhán," he joked.

"I hope that he won't have it for much longer."

"See you Saturday, love."

"Goodnight so."

"Tell Caomhán John Daddy sends his love."

"He never stops talking about you."

"And Bridie, I love you."

"You're drunk all right," she laughed, as she hung up the phone.

John walked out the door of the pub into the rain. He felt he was making a real sacrifice for his family, a pint and a half left on the counter. He sent a few fucks after the car that swished past, splashing him with mud and water from a pothole. He'd a good idea it was Thatch's Porsche. "That one could do with a couple of inches," he said to himself, "to waken a bit of nature in her."

"Fair play to you," Therese said to Bridie as she sat down to dinner. "You must have given him a fair bit of stick. He left the pub with his tail between his legs as soon as he was finished on the phone."

"I wasn't giving out to him."

"Sure you could be heard all over the bar."

"Oh, Lord." Then she noticed that Therese was joking. "You're a right ould shite, you are," she laughed. "Somebody needs to tell him a thing or two. He went back on the drink again yesterday, had an almighty skip, I'd say, that's what he usually means by a couple of scoops."

"Aren't we on it ourselves?" Therese struggled to get the cork from a bottle of wine.

"I said that I'd pay for the next bottle," Bridie chided her.

"This is my treat."

"I feel mean when you get everything like that. I don't like to be under a compliment to anyone. When I have money..."

"I try to do my best for yourself and Caomhán."

"There it is again. What good is doing it, if you're going to cast it up again?"

"I'm not casting anything up. I just said that it's funny that we should complain about John's drinking when we're having a jar ourselves. And you must admit we did have a good skip over the Christmas."

"I don't drink half as much as you do. It wasn't me that spent half this evening in the bar on the way home from work. If you have a problem with it, do something about it. Don't call me a hypocrite."

"OK, so I had a couple of drinks with a client on my way home. I had a hard day. I was worn out from the lack of sleep last night. You might remember some drunken bum on the phone scaring the life out of us. I don't have to make an excuse for having a glass of wine with my dinner."

"Everybody knows how hard you work, how much you've done for the Gaeltacht since you took charge of the Board. They know, because you never stop telling them. Well, the Gaeltacht was there before you came."

"What's got into you this evening, Bridie? Was it something John said? Did he hurt you, insult you?"

"There's nothing wrong with me." She took her own plate, and Caomhán's, gathered up their cutlery, and headed towards the kitchen.

"Leave the dishes. I'll wash them."

"I'll wash them myself."

"I'll dry them so."

"I'll do what I'm paid to do."

"There's no point in talking to you today." Therese sat back and sipped her drink, determined to enjoy her meal and glass of wine.

When she'd washed and dried the dishes, Bridie took Caomhán into his own bedroom and closed the door with a bang. She changed his nappy and put on his all-in-one pyjamas. He refused to be put in his cot without "kiss Teetie." Bridie had to let him go to the kitchen. Climbing up on Therese's knee, he gave her a kiss, but that wasn't enough. He had to have some of her dinner as well. She cut her meat into very small pieces for him. Having tried painstakingly to pick up a piece of meat with the fork and failed, he grabbed a handful and stuffed it into his mouth.

"Hurry up, Caomhán," Bridie shouted from his bedroom.

"Tell Mammy to come up for her own kiss." Therese said it loudly enough to be heard in the room.

"Fuck yourself and your kiss." Bridie was still angry.

"Fuck." There was a glint in Caomhán's eye as he looked up at Therese. Not for the first time it was he who broke the grownup's tension.

"Come on down to bed." Bridie was in the doorway with her hands held out to him. "The things we're teaching you," she smiled.

"I suppose I'll be blamed for that too," Therese said jokingly. As Caomhán was turned away from her, Bridie gave a two finger salute.

"And also with you. In inverted commas," Therese held up four fingers. The tensions dissipated. The three of them spent half an hour playing games, Caomhán hiding, and the women pretending that it was difficult to find him. As he got more and more hyped up, Bridie said, "When fun is best, it's time to rest."

"My mother used to say that," Therese commented.

"You don't often talk about your mother. Do you think about her much?"

"Too much, maybe, especially at Christmas, when everyone else seems to be visiting their families." Therese stood, with folded arms. She'd followed the others to Caomhán's room as he was being tucked into his cot.

"Why don't you go to see them?"

"You know as well as I do."

"Don't you think it's time to forget the past?"

"Do you forget what John did to you?"

"At least I talk to him. And it's only two years since he nearly beat me to death. It's something like twenty years since your father was abusing you. He's old now. Surely the time comes that you have to forgive someone."

"Did he ever say sorry, ever admit what he did to me? Ever show remorse? I don't want anything to do with him, with either of them."

"I heard a priest saying once that the hate you hold in does more damage to you than to the one you hate."

"Spare me the sermon, please, Bridie."

"I'm very wary of John because of what he did to me when we were married, but I can still see him."

"You see him for Caomhán's sake."

"For your own sake I think you should see your parents."

"In case I don't get the legacy," Therese said sarcastically.

"I'd say that you have a lot more than they have."

"I don't really hate my father," Therese mused when they had gone to the sitting-room and Caomhán had settled at last. "I don't hate my mother either, even though she never did anything to stop what was going on. I wouldn't want anything bad to happen to them, or anything like that. If anything I hope that they live longer than I do. I dread their funerals. I was thinking of that when your father was being buried. How I would feel if it was mine? I think I mightn't even go. I don't wish them anything really, good, bad or indifferent. All I want to do is keep my distance."

"You still love them in a way?"

"Maybe I do. I suppose I do. In a way. In a very strange way, but I don't know that love is the right word for it. They brought me into this life. They reared me. They destroyed me, my father especially, even though I blame my mother more because she was too weak to protect me. The harm is done now, and nothing could make black white again. I suppose that they're dead already as far as I'm concerned."

"You don't miss them at all?" Bridie was thinking of the huge gap her father's death had left in her life.

"I miss not having parents, if you know what I mean, people to care for me, for me to care for them, friends to visit at weekends, Christmas. I miss the rapport you have with your parents, the way you and your father could slag each other off, no harm done. I could go to see them, put up a pretence, but that's all that it'd be. The scars are too deep."

"Is it because of that...?" Bridie wanted to ask her question in a way that wouldn't cause hurt or embarrassment. "Is that why you prefer women?"

"Why I'm lesbian? If I am... I don't think so. The experts certainly wouldn't say so. If anything, girls who are abused tend to end up with a man who abuses them in turn. Maybe deep down I'm trying to avoid that, avoid having a relationship with a man who'll batter or abuse me, treat me like my father did. It's much easier to avoid pain than to put yourself through something, for all the pleasure or companionship or even love you might get out of it. I've had too much pain, Bridie. I don't want any more."

"Who does? Well, it's strange that I ended up with a batterer so, even though I was never abused, never beaten apart from a warning smack or two on the bottom. Anyway I don't think anyone seriously goes out looking for a man like that. Deep down inside maybe, there might be something that would draw a woman to a violent man. Maybe they have an animal magnetism because they're violent." Bridie didn't know if she was making sense or not. "I suppose I can't blame John either. I should have had more sense than to marry a man who'd treated me as he did before we were married. I should have seen what alcohol did to him."

"I often wonder is it the alcohol itself that does the damage?" Therese mused, "or does it just bring out the badness that's in us? What's in sober comes out drunk, as the old saying has it."

"The old missionaries were right," Bridie joked. "The devil is in the bottle."

"Bullshit," was Therese's comment on that.

"Didn't you see for yourself. When you uncorked that bottle of wine tonight, the devil came out of it and got into me. I was contrary for no reason at all. I just felt down, I suppose, because John was back on the drink again. And I had to take it out on someone. I wouldn't mind but I felt in grand form while I was talking to him." She gave Therese a pleading look and said quietly, "Sorry about that."

"It doesn't take much to put any of us off our stroke at times, and when you think of how little sleep either of us had last night."

"Devil or no devil, I could have fought with my toenails at one stage this evening. All I needed was some kind of a spark to set me off."

"Leave the devils and the superstition out of it anyway."

"There was a lot of sense in some of them."

"The devil scares me." Therese's brow furrowed.

"Sure you told me a thousand times you don't believe in any of that ould stuff, as you put it, God or devil."

"I don't believe in him, but he still scares me."

"Strange how I often notice that," Bridie said. "People who say they don't believe seem to fear the supernatural more than people who do."

"It sounds reasonable enough to me. I suppose that we all fear the unknown. Someone who believes in an after-life could believe any kind of *seafóid*."

"I don't think Christianity is *seafóid*. In fact I think it's much more sensible than a lot of the stuff you go on with." While she was willing to criticise her own

Church from time to time, Bridie couldn't abide non-believers having a go at religion.

"I was only joking." Therese knew well that it was a sore subject and didn't pursue it further. "Sure we have to talk about something, anything except money."

"They say that money is the cause of most of the problems, even in the very best of marriages."

"Are you calling this one of the best of marriages?"

"It's not the worst," Bridie smiled. "So you do forgive me?"

"For being such a bitch this evening? I do."

"You're not a bad hand at the bitching yourself sometimes."

"Sure I have to stick up for myself," Therese smiled. "No one else will."

"Caomhán doesn't like it when we argue."

"The main thing is not to let it drag on. As the Bible says, 'Do not let the sun go down on your anger'."

"For someone that doesn't believe, you seem to know a lot of the Bible."

"I have to know what the opposition are up to," Therese joked.

"I think there's more to it than that."

"You couldn't avoid religion in the Irish school system. Even if I don't believe it, it doesn't mean that there isn't a lot of sense to some of it. It's part of world literature and history. I don't buy that stuff about virgin birth, or Jesus being the son of God, but there is a lot to be learned in the Bible about life."

Therese collected the bottle of wine and two glasses from the kitchen table. "Now that it's open we'd better not let it go to waste. That's unless you want me to take the pledge," she said, a glint in her eye. She told Bridie that she had to go to London soon to seek more investment for Gaeltacht Board projects. "I'm a bit worried though about you being here on your own with Caomhán. After that phone call last night."

"Don't let me hold back the work of the Board. Can't we stay with my mother?"

"That's right. I never thought of that. That call has driven me paranoid."

"And who will you be staying with in London?"

"Isn't it you that's curious."

"I think I've a right to know."

"Elizabeth Windsor, if you want to know."

"Tell me about her."

"She's middle-aged, married, a bit dowdy, lives in a big house, Buck something."

"You're having me on. The friggin' Queen." Bridie laughed, but quickly became serious. "Have you plans to visit anyone else?"

"My trip is strictly business."

"You must have some girlfriends there."

"You mean I must have been involved with someone?"

"I'm hardly the first and only woman you ever met."

"Things like that shouldn't even be discussed. The past is past. People end up being jealous of somebody else's ghosts."

"So there was someone?"

"I didn't say there was."

"You'd tell me if it was harmless."

"You should be a barrister. You'd be very good at cross-examination, and note that I emphasise *cross*."

"You have to tell me," Bridie said. "You know about John and me."

"It isn't the same at all. I wasn't married to anyone."

"That's not the point. They wouldn't let you marry another woman even if you wanted to. But I'll bet you were involved just as much or more."

"It would be better if I didn't say anything about that part of my life." Therese was very serious. "This is the kind of thing that makes me feel that I'm in competition with John."

"You're not in competition with John. Or if you are you have the competition won." Bridie was persistent. "You have to tell me."

"Curiosity killed the cat. Anyway, it's strictly a business trip. More investment, more jobs, I hope. I don't expect to be wasting my time."

"Nothing else?"

"Don't tell me you're jealous," Therese laughed.

"Tell me about her, so I'll know if I have reason to be jealous or not."

"You don't really want to know."

"What are you trying to hide?"

"Nothing. I didn't know you then. If I did, I wouldn't have looked at anyone else."

"Pull my other leg,"

"The defence rests," Therese said, "as they say in all the best court cases."

"But the prosecution doesn't want to rest."

"You mean the persecution."

"You have to tell me."

"I don't have to do anything."

"Well, I don't like you going over there, without me knowing if you'll be staying with her or not," Bridie insisted.

"You just have to trust me."

"That's not good enough."

"Are you saying that I'm not to be trusted?"

"Are you meeting her or not?"

"No, no, no. There *is* no her." Therese spoke loudly. "There never was. It's not that I didn't have one-night stands, now and again. That was all. It was just a way of satisfying my needs. Physical, sexual, natural needs."

"Don't you think that's wrong?"

"I think it's the most natural thing in the world."

"Why does the Church, all the Churches, I think, condemn it so?"

"When did the Churches understand anything about human nature, human needs, women's needs?"

"Sure they're always talking about the natural law."

"The law they make themselves," Therese said. "I was reared a Catholic too. I know all that stuff. I was so good at Christian Doctrine that they used to call me the nun's pet. But I saw through it all when I left school, and went out in the real world."

"It's hard to imagine you being the nuns' pet."

"I always had, I still have, a lot of time for the nuns. If I believed, I'd like to be a nun. They do the finest of work, some of them anyway. I'm not saying there aren't bitches among them, as there are everywhere."

"What would you do about those physical, sexual, natural needs you were talking about? If you did..." Bridie smiled. "If you do decide to become a nun."

"I have fingers, just like the next person."

"You're awful."

"You ask too many questions."

"So there isn't anyone in London?"

"How many times do I have to tell you? I don't think I had a close friend since I left school until I met you. It's not that I didn't have lots of pals. Even if I say so myself, I was probably the most popular person in the office with both men and women. But close friends, long-term relationships, no." Therese smiled. "So can I go?"

"You'll do what you want anyway."

"I wouldn't want to hurt you, Bridie."

"Ah, you do say the nicest things."

"You're full of shit."

"That's what I mean."

❦

Therese noticed that things were very different at the first post-Christmas meeting of the Gaeltacht Board. The Government-appointed members as well as the elected members from the Government parties opposed almost every proposal she made. That she could take, the cut and thrust of political horse trading. She sensed immediately that the problem was much deeper. Even at a personal level there seemed to be a change of attitude. Most of them trying to avoid her eyes.

When they reached the fourth item on the agenda, Teilifís na Gaeltachta, things got even more poisonous. Those on the Government side said that it was the Minister's opinion that the Chief Executive's proposal for a completely independent service would provide a platform for those who espoused violence. "They'd be free to say anything they want," he said. "It would give the wrong message to the British and the Unionists. They already feel that the Irish language is just another Sinn Féin, IRA propaganda tool."

"There'd be nothing free about it." The Connemara Independent tried to inject a note of humour into the proceedings. "The parties you mention would have to pay for their advertisements, just like everyone else."

"That'd be no problem to them," the Donegal Fine Gaeler answered him. "They'd just rob a few more banks. I'm all in favour of a proper television service, but I don't want it paid for with blood money."

"What the Minister is afraid of," the man from the Meath Gaeltacht said, "is that he wouldn't be able to call the shots himself."

The Connemara Independent made another joke about "calling the shots." "You're really bringing the paramilitaries into it now," he laughed. His attempt at humour was met by a stony silence.

"We have to look at it from the point of view of Northern Unionists," the Galway Fine Gaeler came in to support his Donegal colleague. "If they see the Irish Government putting a propaganda weapon into the hands of the IRA we can forget about any future progress. Why are we giving them this other stick to beat us with, on top of Articles 2 and 3 of our Constitution?"

"I couldn't care less what any Unionist thinks," said a Kerry Fianna Fáiler. "But I think it's stupid to set up a station that hasn't got Government backing. How long is it going to last without state support? I think that it's the Government's duty to provide a proper television service for the people of the Gaeltacht, as well as for all Irish-speaking people. Something with a bit more bite than the mickey mouse couple of hours in the evening we got a few years back."

The Meath man quickly reminded him that his own party was in power when that TV service was set up.

"In partnership," he shot back, "not in real power.

That was all right in its day, a stepping stone until we would get the real thing."

"So you accept stepping stones now?" The Donegal Fine Gaeler harped back to the Anglo-Irish Treaty negotiations of almost eighty years before. "That must be the very very last of the core values of the so-called Party of Reality."

"The Government has been putting it on the long finger for years now." Therese always used the introduction of Civil War politics as a cue to intervene. She added, "An improvement on the existing situation has been promised before every election for the past few years, and we're still waiting for it. It would be in the interest of all political parties to deliver on those promises."

The only woman on the Board was from the Progressive Democrats. She said that the plan impressed her, but she was worried about the type of finance involved. "It looks good on paper, but are there enough business people committed enough to come up with all that advertising revenue? They say that money speaks the seven languages, but I'm not so sure that it speaks Irish. And what about the licence fees? People are notorious for avoiding paying their licences, but the situation will be much worse if Gaeltacht licences are double everyone else's."

"People will pay for something they really want," the bearded Independent said. "Anyone trying to rear a family through Irish knows how badly this is needed. And as far as the business people are concerned, this is a great opportunity to beat the competition, and sell their wares."

Therese produced a sheet of paper with figures and a graph. "Market research shows that a majority of

Irish people have a positive attitude to the Irish language. They may not be always able to speak it, but they're often attracted by Irish labelling or by publicity through the medium of Irish. There's a pride factor, a touch of patriotism involved that is very hard to quantify."

"As a woman does a weekly shopping for a family," the PD member quickly replied, "I'd certainly take more notice of advertising on radio than television. That's what we tend to hear in the kitchen. We don't have time to watch television when there are meals to be prepared and a hundred and one things to be done for a small family. It's in the big supermarkets in town that most people shop, except for smaller items."

"As a woman myself, I can't agree," Therese said.

"Do you do a lot of shopping yourself?" The local bachelor Fianna Fáiler asked her directly, with heavy irony.

"At least as much as you do." There was a time that kind of repartee would have got a laugh. Not today.

The Progressive Democrat woman went on about the fact that it was her party that had brought realism into the question of the country's finances. That was why she had to oppose a project that the Government might have to bail out in the end. "The last thing we need in this country is another white elephant."

"I thought those were an extinct species." Even a Kerryman's quick wit failed to raise a titter of laughter.

"What really gets me," said the Connemara Independent, "is that none of you came up with those objections before Christmas. As far as I was concerned the whole thing was accepted in principle at our last meeting. Was it the turkey that rose in your heads, or what? Or are the big boys in Dublin pulling the strings on their little country puppets?"

"We had the whole holiday to consider it fully." The Kerry Fianna Fáiler didn't think that he was anybody's puppet. It was then that the Independent from out west really put the cat among the pigeons:

"Could all of this have anything to do with the muck-raking rumours that are being spread abroad about our Chief Executive? It'd probably suit a lot of people to get rid of her and put in some party hack in her place."

"Could we stick to the point," The Chairman spoke firmly. "We are discussing Teilifís na Gaeltachta."

"What rumours are you talking about?" The PD woman asked the Connemara Independent.

"You must have your head in the sand altogether if you haven't heard. I personally don't believe them, but even if they're true, I don't think a person's private life has anything to do with their job."

"The image of the Board has to be considered," was the opinion of one of the Government-appointed businessmen.

"Am I on trial here, or something?" Therese asked, "because of some unknown, unstated rumours that circulate in public houses."

The Chairman announced that he was going to adjourn the meeting.

"The last one was adjourned as well," Therese reminded him. "When are we going to get any real business done?"

"I can't see us making any headway here today." The Chairman shrugged his shoulders in exasperation. "It would help if the Chief Executive were to make a statement before the next meeting, denying those very serious rumours. As has been mentioned, the image of the Board has to be considered."

"This is ridiculous," Therese said. "How am I expected to deny rumours that haven't even been stated? Put them on the record, and I'll deal with them."

The silence around the table was broken eventually by the Chairman: "Neither the Minister nor anyone here wants to drag anyone's name through the mud. The Chief Executive has done a very good job. We're all aware of that. She would get every support from the Board if she were to move to the private sector." He spoke directly to Therese. "You'd leave here with what amounts to a golden handshake."

"Do you know where you can put your golden handshake?" She stood up, barely resisting the temptation to stick up her middle finger in a "fuck you" gesture to them all.

"It's worth considering," the Chairman said. "It's a good offer." He then proposed that they adjourn for lunch, and meet again at three o' clock.

"You look like death," was Bridie's greeting when Therese arrived home unexpectedly for her lunch. She normally ate with the Board members on days that there were meetings. She couldn't face them now.

"I'd get sick if I was to sit down to eat with that crowd."

"What's wrong? What have they done?"

"Just hold me," she said, before telling what had happened.

"Tell them where to stick their job," Bridie said. "You don't need them."

"But where did the rumours come from?"

"Maybe there's some peeping Tom about."

"He'd need a very long neck. The bedroom is over

the garage."

"Why don't you sue them?"

"They haven't put anything on the record," Therese replied. "And anyway, you and Caomhán would be dragged into it."

"Don't give in to them."

"The golden handshake is pretty tempting. We could have a nice quiet comfortable life, start a small industry, maybe."

"It's a matter of principle."

"Every principle has a price, Bridie."

"I don't think you're that cynical."

"Why don't the three of us just go away, to London, or someplace?" Therese went to the drink's cabinet and got out the bottle of brandy. "I know that this isn't a great idea in the circumstances, but I want to settle my nerves before going back in there. Will you have a drop?"

"No, thanks, and I don't think we should run away either. That'd look very like an admission of guilt."

"You'd be away from John, and I'd be free of all this hassle."

"Do you think London is the place to rear Caomhán?"

"It'd be better than being here with the other children teasing him about us. Anyway, we could afford to get a place in the country." Therese began to feel giddy after a couple of sips of brandy. "I could fancy myself as part of the stockbroker belt."

"I thought you came back because you wanted to live your life in the Gaeltacht." Bridie tried to bring her back to what she considered reality. "And haven't you often said that you don't give a damn what anyone thinks?"

"Everybody says that until it's themselves that are involved."

"They might have a change of mind by the time you go back to the meeting," Bridie offered hopefully.

"Some of those politicians are like cattle." Therese was very angry with them. "Whatever the party leader or the Minister says is followed to the letter, even if it means swearing that black is white."

"You've very little respect for them."

"Have you?"

Bridie shrugged. "I don't have to deal with them, I'm not in your league."

"I'm not saying that they're bad people as such, or that they don't give some service to the public. What I hate to see is them having to argue against what they believe in themselves, because the other party says the opposite. Opposition for the sake of opposition. And as soon as they get into power they say and do the opposite. There are exceptions, of course, politicians who make use of the party as a tool to help their own people."

"I wonder are those rumours circulating for long," Bridie mused, her mind a long way from politics and politicians. "I'm thinking of something John said, about me not wanting to go back to him because I had you. And Peadar Halloran said something that had the same kind of a double meaning."

"Fuck them." Therese stood up and walked around the table. "Fuck the whole lot of them. It's nobody's business but our own. Jesus, how I hate this narrow-minded, malicious, begrudging, tight-arsed little excuse for a country. It's no wonder that there's so much emigration."

"The same thing happens in every country," Bridie

reminded her. "Private lives have brought down politicians in England and the United States in the last ten years. In Japan as well, I think."

"I've just had a great idea." Therese had not even been listening to her. She left down her glass and punched her left hand with her right fist. "I'll play them at their own dirty game. I'll give as good as I got. If they want innuendo, I'll give them innuendo. I'll have them jumping out the window with all the innuendo." She laughed at her own pun.

"Is that really a great idea?" Bridie wondered was the drink going too quickly to her friend's head.

"I hope the fan is able to take all the shit that's going to hit it this evening." Therese finished her drink. "I'll see you later," she winked.

"Keep the head," Bridie advised.

"Don't worry. Whatever heads are rolling, mine won't be among them."

As soon as the meeting reopened, Thatch took the initiative. "I don't believe medieval witches even got an opportunity to reply to their witch-hunters," she began quietly, "so I'm grateful for this opportunity to reply to the rumour-mongering I was subjected to at the earlier part of this meeting." Standing with her hands pressed flat on the table to hide her nervousness, she continued:

"I gave up a good job in London to come back here to take up this position. I came back, because, as an Irish woman, I wanted to play a practical part in the development and expansion of what I consider the heart of Ireland, the Gaeltacht. I can claim, with justifiable pride, to have been successful in this job. So successful," she paused, to look from face to face, "that I have no intention of accepting a golden or any other coloured handshake. I'm not giving up this job without a fight, and I don't think the people of the Gaeltacht would thank me if I did."

Therese opened a neat cardboard box she had placed on the table in front of her. "I have a file here on each member of the Board," she said. "You might even call it a cupboard of skeletons. It lists those who have taken back-hand bribes to facilitate county council planning permissions. It includes the use of travelling and overnight expenses in order to spend surreptitious nights with lovers. And of course it includes consideration of the Minister's own peccadilloes, often rumoured, never confirmed."

"This is outrageous," the Chairman insisted. "This is completely out of order."

"Everything that was said at this morning's meeting was in order." The bearded Independent relished anything that would upset the established parties. "I don't remember anything being ruled out. No holes barred." He felt that he must be losing his touch. Nobody laughed at his jokes any more. "If we had sauce for the goose before dinner-time, we should have sauce for the ganders now. Throw open the files. I've nothing to hide."

"Would you like me to put some facts on record?" Therese picked up a file. "Shall we start with the Minister?" She was afraid that someone might call her bluff, that she'd have to open the file and display blank pages. "If people want to play dirty," she said, "I'll play dirty too." She replaced the file, closed the box. "Or will we let good sense prevail?"

The Chairman accepted a motion from the Kerry Fianna Fáiler that the Minister should make his views known in writing to the Board before the next meeting.

"After all, his will be the final say. No matter what we decide, he can still veto it." This was considered an honourable compromise for the moment, and the meeting ended.

Therese had been back in her office for about an hour when the Minister rang from his Dublin office. How was she? How had she enjoyed the Christmas? He had heard that there had been some misunderstanding at the Gaeltacht Board meeting. He felt that it was his job to pour oil on troubled waters. "It's quite wrong," he stated, "to suggest that the Government is opposed to the type of television station you've proposed. We accept your plan in principle, but, of course, as guardians of the state finances, we have to be sure of its viability. Why don't the two of us sit down over dinner some evening, Therese, and discuss the possibilities?"

"Well, as I'm sure you have been informed, Minister, the meeting here this morning had more to do with rumour than with policy."

"Rumours," the Minister laughed. "Surely you don't take any heed of the likes of that. I've been the subject of more malicious rumours in my own political career than most. Only for the fact that I have an understanding and loving wife, my marriage would have broken up long ago."

"That would be ironic," Therese couldn't resist the dig, "for a man who took such a prominent part in the anti-divorce campaign."

"Some people have no shame. They'd say anything about you. The dirtier the rumour, the better chance it has of sticking."

"You sound like an expert."

The Minister laughed. "I heard you weren't taking

any prisoners yourself today."

"Do they not play poker in the Gaeltacht?" Therese felt more at ease now, they were speaking each other's language. "Nobody called my bluff."

"They couldn't chance it. They didn't know what you had up your sleeve."

"How can I possibly work with the Board after all this?"

"Let that not worry you. The elected members will soon have to face the electorate, and we'll be appointing some new faces to the other positions. You'll have a new Board virtually in six months time. The Board is expendable. You're not."

"I suppose I can take your word for it, since I've taped our little conversation. I'll be covering my back from now on."

"I wouldn't put it past you. Do you know, Therese, you'd make a great politician. Did you ever think of standing for Dáil Éireann?"

"I suppose you could arrange a nomination?" she joked.

"No problem."

"I don't know that the rumours that are flying about would help."

"Water off a duck's back," he said, in his homely way. "Nine-day wonders don't even last a week now. The media just get their teeth into some other unfortunate. It's a matter of learning to ride out the storms."

"I hear that there's no better man for the ride than yourself," she said with a laugh. But she didn't say it until he'd rung off. He had arranged to meet her at the Gaeltacht Board offices the following Tuesday to discuss the television project.

❧

"John Granny" was Caomhán's new mantra when his father left him home on Saturday evening. He'd brought his son to visit his own mother. Caomhán had obviously enjoyed his day, and fell asleep early on the couch. Bridie carried him down to his cot. She and Therese sat watching television until RTE closed down, the events of the earlier part of the week now like a distant nightmare.

The match was at two o'clock on Sunday afternoon, early because of the shortness of the winter day. It was cold and frosty; fog hung low on the hills. Caomhán was like a little Santa Claus in his all-encompassing red bodysuit. All that could be seen of him was his pudgy face. Even with extra ganseys and coats Bridie and Therese were frozen. But they thought it was important for John to have his son there, even though Caomhán didn't understand what was going on.

"Don't be expecting much from me today," John said when he ran over in his sports gear before the match started. "I'm out of match practice. It's a couple of years since I played Gaelic. It's only a challenge anyway."

"You'll be great," Bridie encouraged him.

The East Galway team they played had a long footballing tradition, although they had fallen on hard times. In the sixties they'd supplied a quarter of the county team. None of them was thought good enough now. They were nevertheless formidable opposition, a worthy test for the newly promoted Rangers.

Their full-back dealt easily with the first few

speculative balls that fell between himself and John, who seemed to be timing his jumps too early.

"He's lost it," Therese heard an old man near her say. "That fellow had the makings of a great footballer if he'd minded himself." She was more interested in the crowd reaction than in the game itself. She was thinking ahead. Games like this would go down a treat on the new television station. There could be community involvement, cameras and microphones to pick up facial expressions, witty comments.

The play was at the other end of the pitch for nearly ten minutes, and the visitors tacked on four points as the home team floundered. Then the new schoolteacher caught a short kick-out and lashed the ball high in the air between full-back and full-forward standing on the edge of the square.

"Low ball for John," someone shouted. "He's not a friggin' seagull." This time John made no attempt to catch the ball. He fisted it neatly back above his head and over the bar. His team seemed to suddenly grow in confidence. They scored one point from play, another from a free, a third from a forty-five. These were quickly cancelled by a fairly soft goal at the other end when their goalkeeper, unsighted by the winter sunlight, let an easy lob in over his head.

"That fellow couldn't catch a cold," was one comment. "He wouldn't stop a clock." Therese had her notebook out. This side of the game was never covered by the media. She jotted down ideas she intended to present to the head of programming.

John caught the next ball that came in his direction on his chest, dummied the full-back and sent a scorcher of a shot in the direction of the goal. The goalkeeper made a fine one-handed save. He tipped it over the bar, soccer style, at the expense of a point.

"Change goalies and we'll bate the daylights out of ye." An echo from the Battle of the Boyne: "Change kings and we'll fight you all over again."

Immediately after that, the Rangers left-half-back soloed fifty yards before popping over a fine individual point. The locals were one point down at the change of ends.

The second half was barely a minute old when John had the ball in the net. He followed a ball that seemed to be going wide out to the corner. An elbow in the ribs took care of the full-back, who had been sticking to him like a leech. The referee didn't see or maybe want to see the foul; the same full-back had the reputation of being an iron-hard man.

The corner-back came off his man to stop John as he soloed along the end line. He passed to the man left unmarked, who transferred the ball back to him at speed. There was only the goalkeeper to beat. He did it with a neat flick of the ball over his head into the far corner. "It's an ill wind," John thought, as he ran back to face the kick-out, applause and cheers ringing in his ears. It was from playing soccer in the prison yard with the Cockneys he had learned that particular trick to fool a goalie.

"Fair play to you, John, you never lost it," the old man who'd criticised him earlier shouted.

He didn't score again for the rest of the match. He didn't need to. Anyway he felt shagged. He hadn't run as much in years. The opposition didn't realise that. They brought their best player back from midfield to mark him. Because he was given so much attention, the rest of the forwards began to run riot. They

eventually ran out relatively easy winners by five
points.

There was a great atmosphere in the pub afterwards,
the two teams and their supporters mixed easily
together, English and Irish were spoken. There was
talk, laughter, music. Caomhán enjoyed the
commotion. He was trying to dance in the middle of
the floor when John was carried in shoulder-high. His
son was raised up on his father's shoulders while he
himself was high in the air. They were let down to
earth when the pub owner came out to present his
own challenge cup to the winners.

The cup was filled with a mixture of whiskey and
cider. It was passed around from person to person.
Bridie's heart fell when she saw John drink from the
cup. She'd have let that go if she hadn't seen a double
whiskey beside the pint of cider he was trying to pass
off as non-alcoholic Cidona. She sipped both of his
drinks to make sure.

"It's not too easy to fool you," he laughed.

"It's not me that's the fool," she answered him
coldly. "Come on, Caomhán, we're going home."

"What's your hurry?"

"You told me you were off the drink."

"For fuck's sake. I never played as well in my life as
I did out there. I deserve some reward."

"I gave you a choice, the booze or Caomhán." He
followed them to the car, but Bridie refused to open
the window to listen to his pleas.

"Don't you think you're a bit hard on him?"
Therese asked, as she drove away.

"He's had his chances." Bridie was looking out the
side window, seeing nothing as the car sped along.
After some time she broke the silence. "I thought

you'd be the last person in the world to defend him."

"It's just that I think there's a time and a place..."

"It's a bit of support I'd expect."

"It was a big day for him."

"I supported you when you were under pressure the last day."

"You're right about the drink, Bridie, but is a pub the place for a confrontation?"

"There's never a right place."

"There is. At the house. When you're on your own ground."

"I don't ever want to see him again."

"A father is entitled..."

"Let him get a solicitor, go to court. He's had chance after chance and he's blown them all."

"What'll you do when he lands on the step this evening? Or next Saturday? Or whenever?"

"I'll ignore him, let him wait there until he rots."

"Until he kicks in the door, more likely."

"Well, will you tell him I don't want to see him?" Bridie asked.

"If that's what you want."

"That's the sort of support I need, not someone making excuses for him."

"I won't be here during the week."

"I'm talking about this evening, tonight. I'm going to a solicitor tomorrow, to send a letter, tell him to stay away. I want to find out about barring orders."

They had just parked at the front of the house when another car pulled up behind Therese's.

"It's him," Bridie said. "Tell him I don't want to see him." She got out of the car, ran up the steps and in the front door. Therese loosened the straps on Caomhán's safety belt and lifted him from the baby-chair. John was standing close to her when she straightened up, Caomhán in her arms.

"I want to see her," John said.

"You mean Bridie?"

"I want to see my wife."

"She doesn't want to see you." Therese wanted to avoid a scene. "Not this evening anyway."

"Well, when can I fucking see her?" he asked loudly. Therese felt Caomhán press against her, frightened. She backed away.

"Why don't you let things cool down a bit, John?" She slowly climbed the steps as she spoke, wishing she was inside the door. Safe. John put out his hands:

"Caomhán, come to John. Come to John Daddy."

Caomhán looked at him before quickly putting his arms around Therese's neck and turning away. John ran up the steps as they went in the front door. Bridie slammed it shut and put on the safety lock. He hammered at the door. Then they heard someone from the car talking to him. Looking out the window they saw a man leading him down the steps by the sleeve of his jacket. John stood for a moment looking up at the house before getting in beside the driver.

John went back to the after-match celebration in the pub. He accepted congratulations, had his back slapped, smiled at well-wishers, but his mind was far away. He was planning how he would "get" Thatch. The bloody bitch had turned Caomhán against him.

"I'd love to fuck the living daylights out of her," he told himself, not for the pleasure it would give her but for the pain. He'd ram her until she'd split in two. No name he could think of, whore, slut, cunt, any of the rest of them was good enough for her. She was the pits. He'd get her. He'd get her all right.

He thought of burning down the house over her head, but that was out of the question. Not with Bridie and Caomhán there. He knew now that Bridie was in no way to blame for any of this. Her head had been turned, her mind changed. Wasn't it obvious that she'd fallen for him again that time her father died? Until the other one got her filthy claws in her, turned her against him.

It was then the thought struck him. He would hit her where it hurt most. In the pocket. He'd burn down the Gaeltacht Board offices, put her out of a job. But they'd get him, jail him. What the fuck? He'd go in the sea. Life wasn't worth living anyway, not with Caomhán turned against him, Bridie refusing to talk to him. "I'll get the bitch even if it kills me. I'll go out in a blaze of glory."

He excused himself from the company as if he was going to the toilet. Micil always left the keys in his banger. John sat in and drove away. He filled the tank to the top at the Texaco station. He asked for a plastic container of petrol as well. He was going fishing in the morning, he said, he needed it for the outboard. Money was no object now, he wouldn't be around much longer.

He rang the fire brigade, reported a forestry fire back near Maam. He rang again a few minutes later, said there was a chimney fire in Athenry near a petrol station. They'd guess these were hoaxes, but they'd have to check them out anyway. It'd give the fire in Furbo time to get a grip.

His plans had a bit of a setback as he approached

the Gaeltacht Board building. It was a great big fortress of concrete and glass. How was he to get in, start the fire? Only for the steps he could crash the car in through the front door, light it up and run. He drove around the back. There was a pre-fab wooden building in the car park. That'd help get things going.

Micil would get more than the car was worth from the insurance. John backed it up against the wooden building and doused petrol from the plastic container on the seats. He spilled a trail of petrol from the pre-fab to the main building, smashed a window and threw in the half-full container.

John hadn't reckoned with the speed with which petrol lights. He had barely struck the match when there was a whoosh and a blinding flash. He fell flat on his back, his face singed in the heat. Then he realised his clothes were on fire. He jumped up, tore off his pullover as he ran to a grassy slope and rolled over and over. He thought he was free of the fire until he felt the pain in his leg. His trousers were still burning. He was pulling them off when the car exploded. He didn't remember anything else until he woke up in hospital. His mother was sitting at the bedside saying her Rosary.

At the other side of the bed a nurse was fixing up some kind of a drip. She smiled at him. "You're lucky."

There was a white sheet across him. He could see his feet. They looked all right. Most of his left leg was bandaged, as were his hands. The rest of him seemed to be undamaged.

"You're a disgrace." His mother started as soon as the nurse went out through the curtains.

"Not now, Mam. I feel awful. What happened?"

"What happened? You nearly put half the

THE COMPELLING AND UNFORGETTABLE SAGA OF THE CALVERT FAMILY

| April £2.95 | August £3.50 | November £3.50 |

From the American Civil War to the outbreak of World War I, this sweeping historical romance trilogy depicts three generations of the formidable and captivating Calvert women – Sarah, Elizabeth and Catherine.

The ravages of war, the continued divide of North and South, success and failure, drive them all to discover an inner strength which proves they are true Calverts.

Top author Maura Seger weaves passion, pride, ambition and love into each story, to create a set of magnificent and unforgettable novels.

W🌐RLDWIDE

THREE UNBEATABLE NOVELS FROM
W●RLDWIDE